Collision Course

Short Fiction
By
David Boyer

Table Of Contents

Creepy Crawl

Reflections

Poor Larry

Sara Has A Monkey On Her Back

Jack and Norma Jean

The Things We Leave Behind

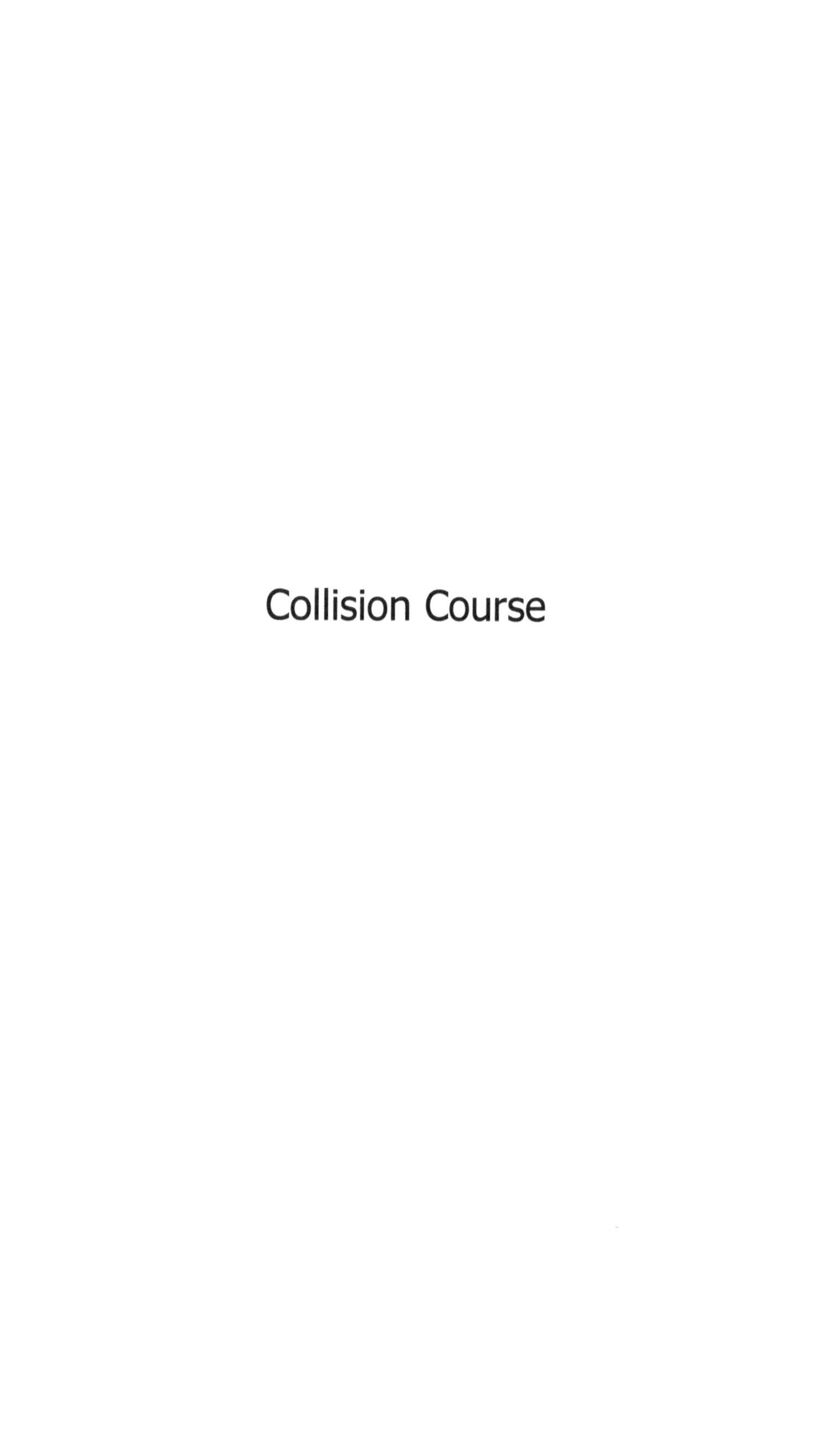

Collision Course

Creepy Crawl

Milo thought he'd hit the jackpot.

The proverbial pot of gold at the end of the magical rainbow.

H'ed been casing the home for weeks, day and night, watching the pretty rich family come and go, knew their schedules, had their whole life pretty much down to a science; the husband left for work around 7:50 am, the wife around 8:25 am, and the teenage daughter around 9 am – for the first shift at a local hamburger joint.

Then later in the day, the family would adjourn to the patio out back for some takeout food and cheerful banter and a dip in the pool before going back inside for some TV and then bedtime.

Just your average but wealthy valley residents who would hide their money and guns in a safe in the bedroom, and their jewels in sock drawers to throw potential burglars off.

But Milo had been in the business long enough to know all of the good stash spots and it normally didn't take him long to find them and be out before anyone was the wiser.

It was no different tonight; as he crept around in the semi darkness of the living room, he immediately spotted the owner's extensive album collection;

Jefferson Airplane, Crosby, Stills, Nash, and Young, and Steppenwolf. *Good taste in music,* he thought, *but bad taste in décor.*

The furniture and wall paintings, like a lot of the styles of the late 60s, were ugly and gawdy at best. No way to sell them, unless it was to a collector, and Milo had no connections in such social circles.

As he swung his small flashlight beam around the dining room, he could see a painting hanging right above the dining table that looked as though someone had dumped a can of red paint on a blank canvas and let their dog rub his hind quarters all over it.

But as he just shook his head in disbelief and turned to walk toward the nearby staircase, something out of the corner of his eye caught his attention; the bottom corner of the gawdy red painting was smeared with hair.

No, not hair; fur.

Animal fur.

Milo couldn't tell what species of animal it was, but he knew that wealthy families that lived in upscale neighborhoods normally didn't own paintings that were scrawled in blood and matted with fur, so he knew that he had just broken into a home where something *very* bad and weird had happened, and he didn't want to be here anymore.

But it was too late.

He heard whispers, and then muffled footsteps.

Like someone was walking around close by, barefoot.

The first voice was female. It said, *Did you see that?*

Then another female voice. *What?*

Then a male voice. *Patty, you been popping acid again?*

The first female voice again. *No, I ain't been popping anything. I saw a light.*

Milo immediately shut his flashlight off and slipped it into the pocket of his jacket, backing up into the shadows. Then the male voice again; *I didn't see a damn thing. Linda, you take Patty and go upstairs. I'm gonna look down here.*

There was no response; just the muffled sound of footsteps retreating up the nearby staircase, and then, *nothing*.

Except for the mild ticking of a grandfather clock nearby, Milo couldn't hear anything. It was so sudden, too, like with the departure of the two females, any and all other sounds just vanished, bled off the face of the Earth and all that was left was the muffled sound of Milo's own shallow breathing, minimal air reaching his lungs, not wanting to make a sound to alert his fellow thieves of his presence.

After a several more labored breaths, Milo gently stepped out of the shadows, tip-toeing it through the darkness, silently praying that he wouldn't step on anything that would make even a modicum of noise.

He couldn't see anything but the darkness, which seemed to be swallowing him up now, like a shark would slide effortlessly and unnoticed up through the depths of the ocean and swallow it's victim whole; *chomp- chomp- gulp!* - and down you go.

The very thought of what awaited him if he was caught by three people who would kill a family pet and smear it's guts all over a wall painting made his stomach tighten up in knots now, his breathing even more labored and his bladder loosening up on him.

He knew he had to get out of there – and quickly.

#

One thing Milo had to his advantage was, he could *smell* his fellow thieves when they were nearby.

The only way he could describe it, in his mind, was the odor of an old wet, stray dog, either that or a human being that hadn't bathed in weeks in the dead heat of a California summer.

The odor was extremely unpleasant, almost sickening, but at least he knew when they were close by – and he was smelling it *now*.

Ducking into a nearby bathroom, Milo hopped into the shower, gently pulled the shower curtain closed, took a deep breath, exhaled – and waited.

Then, a voice.

Patty's voice.

She said, *Tex? Where are you?*

A male voice. *In the downstairs laundry room. Why don't you just tell the whole damn neighborhood? WHISPER, remember?*

Then the other female voice, Linda. *Charlie says we're supposed to creep crawl. Don't make any noise.*

Patty said, *I AM whispering!*

Tex said, *Both of you, SHUT THE HELL UP! I gotta do everything.*

Patty said, *I gotta pee.*

Tex said, *Well, make it fast, we gotta be outa here soon, ladies.*

Then Milo heard the bathroom door being slammed open, the toilet seat being lifted, and the sound of someone grunting as they urinated. The smell of the urine and the body odor almost made Milo sick, but he kept his composure, held it down, even as bile filled his throat.

Then he heard the sound of the toilet flushing, and he breathed a sigh of relief.

But not for long.

Believing Patty had left the bathroom, Milo began to pull the shower curtain back when he saw that Patty hadn't left the bathroom yet, and was standing in front of the mirror, looking at herself. He quickly pulled the curtain back and stood peeking through a small slit in the plastic.

Patty was leaned over the sink, staring into her own reflection, into her vacant, bloodshot eyes, at the dirty, blemished skin, and filthy, greasy hair.

For her, it was like staring into an empty shell; a face of madness, something that *used* to be human.

She opened her mouth now, looking at her teeth – or what was left of them. At seeing some of her jagged, broken front teeth, Milo could envision those nasty, germ infested teeth biting into his flesh, giving him rabies or some other nasty disease. He shuddered and blocked the vision from his head as best he could.

That's when it happened.

As he stood peeking at her through the tiny slit in the curtain, she looked away from her own reflection to see his own tiny eyeball peeking through that tiny little slit, and she went ballistic.

Wheeling around like a whirling dervish, she practically leapt into the air like a jungle cat, digging her long, dirty fingernails into the curtain, but Milo had already ducked to one side, catching her in mid air, and wrapped his strong arms around her, one arm underneath her rib cage, and the other arm around her throat, squeezing hard, cutting off her air supply.

She was unconscious within seconds.

He gently lowered her limp body into the shower, closed the curtain behind him, and slipped out of the bathroom, gently closing the door behind him, and disappeared into the darkness again, not sure of which way to go next.

#

Several minutes later, Tex and Linda stood down the hallway from the first floor bathroom, Tex becoming more angry by the second.

Lighting a cigarette, he said to Linda, *Go tell your friend to hurry up so we can get the hell out of here.*

Linda said, *It's not my turn to babysit her. Charlie said YOU are in charge.*

Tex shook his head and said, *You stupid bitch. I'm gonna tell Charlie when we get back to the ranch.*

Ignoring the instant barrage of obscenities spewing from Linda's mouth, Tex turned to walk down the hallway with Linda right behind him, flipping him the bird behind his back.

Upon entering the bathroom, Tex could tell Patty had been there; dirty handprints on the sink, and dirty footprints on the floor tiles. He had wondered at times how Charlie could ever be aroused by a woman with such poor personal hygiene, then again, he had no room to be judgemental.

As he swung his tiny flashlight beam around the room, it landed on a dirty little foot hanging out of the shower stall, partially wrapped in plastic. Looking closer, he immediately reached down and yanked the plastic away to find Patty lying in there unconscious, her blank eyes fixed on the stall wall.

He grabbed her foot and shook her, while Linda spoke to her, trying to get her to wake up. It was no use for now; she was out cold. Seeing she was still breathing, Tex said, *She's okay for now. We got other shit to take care of.*

Seemingly clueless, Linda said, *Like what?*

Tex said, *Look at the red welts on her neck, dumbass. Somebody used a choke hold on her. We got to find out WHO used a choke hold on her.*

Linda said, *Yeah! We'll mess them up! Charlie will like that!*

Grinning, Tex said, *You're damn right he will. You take the ground floor and I'll look up here.*

With a big smile, Linda said, *What if I find them first?*

He said, *Save some for me, I want to have some fun, too.*

#

Milo could hear the muffled voices again, somewhere nearby, but otherwise, nothing but the eerie silence and pitch black darkness and the ocassional flash of lightning through the windows.

There was a strong storm brewing out there, but he knew it would be nothing compared to the shitstorm that would be brewing in the home he was trapped in for now.

As he crept quietly along on the second floor

landing, he glanced up to see a possible means of escape; a balcony, right outside the master bedroom.

If he could just crawl over the edge and scale down the long rosebush trellis, he could be long gone before anyone even knew he'd been there. It might be a sharp, prickly trip down, but the thought of a few thorns in his ass seemed pale in comparison to what the creepy folks inside might have in store for him.

So, the balcony it was.

#

As he slowly and carefully maneuvered his way down then trellis, Milo was still being jabbed and pierced by rose bush thorns, several of the tiny wounds so deep that he almost cried out in pain and frustration, but he held his tongue in fear of what may be waiting for him below.

Blood streaming into his eyes now from a wound on his scalp, he was momentarily blinded by a veil of blood until he stopped, righted himself, and used his left hand to wipe the blood from his eyes.

As he began descending the trellis again, he looked down to see he only had about eight feet left to go before he was level with the hedges, and breathed a momentary sigh of relief.

That is, until the gunshot rang out.

A small patch of the rosebush below him suddenly exploded, sending rose petals cascading down as he wheeled his head around to see Linda standing on the patio below, aiming a small, .22 caliber revolver at him.

Before she could fire again, he made the painful choice to drop the remaining eight feet to the ground, landing in the hedges, knocking the wind right out of him.

As he lay in the shrubbery gasping for breath, he noticed a small – but very sharp – garden trowel, snatched it up in his right hand, and waited.

He could hear Linda's shallow breathing as she move closer, heard the hammer being cocked on the .22, and then he could *smell* her, and knew she was close enough for him to end this charade right here and now.

Taking a deep breath, he lunged out of the hedges, to see her face almost level with his own, and jammed the tip of the trowel deep into her stomach, cruelly twisting it as she slowly dropped to her knees, her bloodshot eyes full of pain and terror.

She sat there on her knees for a few seconds, in silence, staring right into Milo's eyes, mouthed several words Milo couldn't understand, then fell face forward into the hedges and lay still.

Milo quickly snatched up the .22 and checked the chamber; three bullets left.

He tucked it into his waistband and turned to disappear into the darkness, then stopped in his tracks, looking back at the home stocked full of all sorts of great stuff to sell on the black market.

And that album collection? He just *had* to have it.

So, back inside he went.

#

Tex had heard the gunshot.

He ran through the home and toward the patio to see the outline of a human body lying near some shrubbery. Gently sliding the patio door open, he stepped outside just far enough to see what – who – it was – lying there in a pool of blood; Linda.

He knew she was dead; it's in the eyes.

He also knew Charlie would be furious if Tex didn't exact some from of revenge against the asshole that killed her, too.

He slid the patio door shut, locked it behind him, and, pulling a large hunting knife from his waistband, he slowly crept back into the darkness, sniffing the air like a blood hound.

#

In the downstairs bathroom, Patty was just now waking up, still dizzy and disoriented.

As she slowly sat up in the stall and shook her head to clear it, she heard the sound of the bathroom door creaking open. She placed both of her hands on the stall walls, stood straight up, her eyes searching the stall for anything she could use as a weapon.

There was nothing.

Shit! She thought, feeling defeated. Then she thought, *Screw it, I don't need a weapon. I'll rip his throat out with my teeth if I have to. NOBODY messes with Patty. Even Charlie says so.*

Hearing the door opening all the way now, the edge of the door leaning against the edge of the shower stall, she took a deep breath, exhaled, and yanked the shower curtain aside, her eyes wild and her teeth bared like a fox trapped in a culdesac.

There was Milo, standing there with the .22 pointed right at her face. The tension in her frail body all but gone now, her face softened as she said, "Where did you get that gun?"

Cocking the hammer back, Milo said, "I took it from your friend. Your *dead* friend, that is."

Her dirty face forrowed into a frown again as she said, "Tex will get you for this. He'll skin you alive and make sure you suffer."

Milo snickered and said, "I can't wait to meet him."

She said, "You won't feel that way when he's slicing you up like beef jerky. Charlie would love *that*, too."

Milo sighed and said, "Are you finished now? I have things to do."

She said, "Like dying?"

He said, "Any last words?"

She spit at his feet and said, "You don't have the *balls* to do it."

He pulled the trigger, sending her flying back against the stall wall, a bullet in her forehead.

He said, "Tell Charlie I said hello."

#

Tex was back on the first floor now, creeping through the dining room, doing his best to stay within the shadows.

A storm was hitting full force now, the heavy rain pelting the roof and windows like bullets and the wind howling like a lonely ghost.

Each time lightning would flash through the window glass, he would look around to see if he could spot anything out of the ordinary – like the shadow of a man carrying a gun – but so far he'd seen nothing.

But he could *smell* Milo.

Smell his sweat, his fear.

Tex had lived like an animal – lived among the animals of our society – for so long, he'd learned to act like them, adapt to their way of life, his human senses now as acute as a wild animal.

He could smell Milo, knew he was close by.

But Milo could smell him, too.

Neither of them knew it, but they were only one room away from each other; Milo in the living room, huddled down by the album collection, and Tex in the dining room, huddled down against the wall.

Except for brief flashes of lightning and bouts of thunder, all that could be heard was the ticking of the grandfather clock - *tick tock tick tock* – and the faint but audible sound of their own shallow breathing.

Milo knew he couldn't allow this insane charade to carry on much longer.

There was a terrible storm brewing outside.

It was only several hours until daylight.

Milo had no idea of when the family that lived there would be back from vacation.

It was now or never.

Milo said into the darkness, "You know, we could just end this right now; you leave, and nobody else has to die."

There was no immediate reply, just some barely audible breathing, then Tex said, "You kill Patty too, you son of a bitch?"

Lighting a cigarette, Milo said, "She gave me no other choice."

Tex said, "Well, just maybe I ain't got no other choice than to kill you, too."

Milo said, "Fair enough. But I wouldn't count on it, friend."

Tex said, "If Charlie was here? You'd already be dead."

Milo said, "Well, apparently your buddy Charlie isn't here, so it's just you and me, isn't it?"

There was a long, uncomfortable silence between them, and Tex said, "Well, Charlie is supposed to be here soon."

Milo provided no reply; he had already sniffed out Tex's current location, and was rounding the corner, right behind him, in the dining room. All he could see was a shadow – a silhouette – a few feet in front of him, but that's all he needed.

Tex said, "I can hear you, asshole." Then the silhouette stood upright, brandishing a large hunting knife. Milo could see his own reflection in the blood stained blade, and knew it was time.

Milo raised the .22 and aimed it at the back of Tex's head, and said, "And I can *SEE* you."

Then he pulled the trigger.

#

By the time Milo had packed up the album collection, any money or jewelry he could find, and a bottle of some really good single malt scotch, the sun was coming up over the horizon.

As he walked down the hill behind the home to pack the last of his ill gotten booty into the trunk of his Jaguar, he suddenly realized that the full impact of what had happened over the last few hours hadn't even hit him yet.

After placing the album collection in the trunk and closing it, he leaned against the driver's door and lit a cigarette, and sampled the scotch, taking a short break before leaving.

Almost twenty minutes later, the sun beating down on him now, he was still sipping the scotch and chain smoking Pall Malls. He couldn't help but feel as though there was something missing...something he hadn't quite accomplished just yet.

Tex had said, *Well, Charlie is supposed to be here soon.*

A painting smeared with animal blood.

A house full of animalistic subhumans.

Milo checked the chamber of the .22; there was one shot left.

Call it morbid curiosity, or maybe even providing a much needed public service. Maybe it was his fate, or even his destiny.

He took one more sip of scotch, dropped the bottle on the ground, slipped the revolver back into his waistband, and walked back up to the house.

Charlie would be there soon.

Reflections

I'll never forget the first time I killed a man.

Wait...I'm getting way ahead of myself calling it a killing. Yes, I did kill him, but you couldn't really classify it as a murder. I shot him in order to save an innocent person's life, in the line of duty.

I used to be a cop.

Well, I'm still a cop, but I guess I just don't feel like one. A righteous cop, anyway.

I almost lost everything.

#

It was a justified shooting – a young man by the name of Tommy Ray Wallace.

To say that Tommy was born on the wrong side of the tracks was putting it mildly.

Born to an alcoholic, prostitute mother and a father with a violent criminal background, Tommy had quickly become the poster boy for a dysfunctional family and child abuse.

By the time he was thirteen-years-old, he had already spent six months in a juvenile detention center for vandalism, theft, and killing a neighbor's dog with a baseball bat. Upon his release, the first thing he'd done was shoplift a bottle of liquor and gone on another violent rampage, this time attacking the liquor store's owner, choking him into unconsciousness.

And he was just getting started.

#

His short, pathetic life came full circle at the age of seventeen, when, upon returning to his parent's home to retrieve some of his clothing, walked in on his mother having sex with a strange man and had proceeded to beat him within an inch of his life.

The man survived – barely – and, in fear for his life, had declined to press charges against Tommy. His mother, though, was a different story altogether. Feigning concern for her only son's welfare and that of the general public, she did press charges against him, and he was sent back to the detention center again, and after his eighteenth birthday, was transferred to a prison for the remainder of his five year sentence.

Due to prison overcrowding, he was paroled after serving only three years of his original sentence, and upon his release, went straight back to his parent's home and proceeded to kill both of them with his father's own handgun.

Then he was in the wind.

That's when we met – for the first and last time.

#

I had been patrolling the East end of Bloomington – known fondly by local, law-abiding residents as "the Wild East End" - a community of dilapidated trailer parks, ancient, abandoned homes that had been turned into meth labs, two liquor stores, and a pool hall – slash – bar and grill that mainly catered to drug dealers, rednecks, alcoholics, and lonely hearts looking for love in all the wrong places.

I was sitting at a stoplight, lighting a cigarette and rolling my window down when the call came through about Tommy.

Having no prior, first-hand knowledge of Tommy or his pathetic past, I shifted the cruiser into high gear and headed toward the East end only a few blocks away. Big tough guy cop who loves old Clint Eastwood Dirty Harry flicks headed toward his destiny and all that good shit.

I had absolutely *no* idea of what awaited me once I got there.

Then again, Tommy had no idea it was going to be his last day on Earth, either.

When I pulled into the liquor store parking lot, there was Tommy, standing there holding a young woman by throat with one hand and using his free hand to press the blade of a large hunting knife against her carotid artery. The fear in her eyes was so *real*, nothing like you see in the movies. No Hollywood actress could ever pull this look off as well as a *real* victim of violent crime.

One of the first things I noticed as I jumped out of the cruiser was the absence of anyone else in the parking lot but me, Tommy, and the young woman he was holding captive. No other customers, no other cops, *nobody*. It was as though time had stood still for us, everything moving in slow motion, like the three of us were caught up in some kind of time warp.

And the only way out was going to be to shoot Tommy.

He had a wild, crazy, I'll-go-down-dead-before-you-take-me sort of look in his eyes, and the woman was screaming at the top of her lungs, a deafening, high-pitched, piss-your-pants type of scream that would have put any B-horror film actress to shame.

I already had my service weapon pulled and was poised in the standard defensive position, my shoulders squared, my feet about shoulder length apart, my Glock aimed right at his forehead. I couldn't get a good heart shot, with the woman blocking my view.

"Drop the knife and let the girl go, asshole!" I screamed, doing my best bad-ass cop impression. You had to let them know you meant business, and you wouldn't think twice about blowing their brains out. If you let them see fear in *your* eyes, they would play on that, have the upper hand. You had to be just as crazy – if not more crazy – than they are.

He didn't even bat an eye. He had the wild eyes going on, but otherwise spoke very calmly, as though my threatening his life hadn't fazed him a bit. He was actually grinning. He said, "I don't think so, asshole. Drop that gun or I'll cut this bitch's head off." He pressed the blade against her throat just hard enough to draw a bead of blood, and upon feeling the blood streaming down her neck, she woman began screaming even louder now, losing her mind.

I stepped two feet closer, for a better head shot. I said, in the most stern, authoritative tone I could muster,

"I said, drop the knife, or I'll be forced to shoot you. Last chance."

His response was to press the blade even harder against her throat, drawing even more blood, and she flew into a blind panic then, screaming and squirming to get free of his grip, endangering her own life even further.

That's when I took the shot.

My aim was true. The bullet struck Tommy right between the eyes, sending him sprawling backward, the girl falling with him, landing right on top of him. She immediately began scampering away from him, on her hands and knees, still screaming like a banshee. I ran to her and tried to calm her down her but she was too far gone by then to hear anything I said.

She never thanked me for saving her life, either. Imagine that.

#

Yet...I couldn't get the shooting out of my mind. Had trouble finding any real justification for his death at my hands. They say some cops can handle the guilt and some can't. I guess I could be classified in the latter category.

The memory of that day was always with me. It hung over me like a death shroud, a constant cloud cover that was always blocking out the sun. Even on the most beautiful day I would feel dark and dreary and deeply depressed – and, at one point, even suicidal.

My wife was the first to notice my mood swings and overall change in my daily routine. My personal hygiene began to suffer, and my eating habits and sleeping habits changed dramatically over a very short period of time. Thank God my kids were still too young at the time to pick up on it. Or maybe they had picked up on it, but were patient with me in hopes that someday they would no longer have to watch their father fall apart before their eyes.

Then, in the midst of all my personal pain and turmoil, I was at the liquor store one day – the same liquor store where I'd taken Tommy's life in the parking lot – and lo and behold, there was his grandmother, Pearl, perched on an old lawn chair in the side lot, staring holes through me as I exited the store with a carton of cigarettes.

I'd seen her picture in the newspaper way back when the details of the shooting had made the front page. ***Courageous Cop Saves Woman's Life***, the headline had read. ***Local Career Criminal's Reign of terror Comes To An End***, read another.

And right below the article, a picture of Tommy's grandmother, her eyes wet with tears, telling *her* side of the story, about how some rookie cop trying to make a name for himself had shot her only grandchild in cold blood.

The second I saw her I made it a point to look away and make a mad dash for my used Chevy Malibu with worn out tires and expired plates when, undeterred by my attempt to avoid her, she said, "You...you're the one who shot my grandson."

Instead of jumping into my car and hightailing it out of the lot, for some reason, call it guilt or morbid curiosity or a glutton for punishment or what-not, I stopped dead in my tracks, and turned to face her down.

Swallowing the lump in my throat, I said, "Excuse

me?"

She squirmed around in the lawn chair, lit a Pall Mall non-filter, and said, "I said, you're the one who shot my grandson. I recognized you, alright." She dragged off her cigarette and continued. "You look...*different*, now. Don't look so good. I always heard a guilty conscience will do that to a man."

Lighting a cigarette myself, I replied, "It was a justified shooting. He would have killed that girl...I could see it in his eyes."

Flipping her cigarette butt into the bushes nearby, she retorted, "That what they call it now? Justified? He had a knife, you had a gun. Wasn't no contest there. Besides, I know – *knew* – my grandson. He was just blowing smoke up your ass, acting all tough. He wouldn't have *really* killed that girl. He just wanted you to *think* he would have."

I said, without thought or hesitation, "Well, he should have thought about that before he got drunk and crazy and took a hostage, huh?"

Lighting another cigarette, she said, "It was me that had to identify the body, his mama wasn't around to do it. You know why he shot her, his own mama?"

I had a very good idea why Tommy had thought shooting his own mother was justified, but out of curiosity as to why his grandmother thought so, I said, "No, enlighten me."

She said, "You didn't read his record? That's hard to believe. Anyway, I was all he had left, and I could only do so much, in my condition. Ever hear of COPD, Mr tough guy?"

I said, "So...you think chain smoking is going to help your condition?"

"Better than my grandson's current condition, ain't it?" she said, puffing away again. "You ever smelled a dead body, Mr hero?"

I had, more than once. There's no other smell like it. You could often tell just how long someone had been dead just by the stench. Imagine a pound of rancid, rotting hamburger. Then *multiply* that by *each* pound, say up to one-hundred and fifty to two-hundred pounds. Then add in some maggots, flies, body gases, and seeping body fluids. And often times, upon death, a person's bladder and bowels let go at the time of death, adding even more rancid odor to the mix. Oh yes...there is no other smell like it in the world.

Feeling a little queasy, I said, "Yes, of course. I'm a cop." As good an answer as any, I'd thought, under the circumstances.

She lit another cigarette and said, "That's the way my grandson smelled, when I went to ID the body. Can you imagine that? His grand-mama standing there, smelling that awful smell and looking at the big hole in his head?"

No, I thought, glumly. *I couldn't imagine having to ID one of my own kids or grandkids and having to smell that*. But what I said was, "I'm sorry, lady, really I am. But like I said, it *was* a justified shooting, and I saved someone's life in the process. It was, what I refer to as, a win- win situation, in the end."

She flipped her cigarette into the bushes again and said, "You just keep on thinking that, Mr hero. You keep on fooling yourself into thinking it was a righteous kill. Keep on thinking that each and *every* time you pop open another bottle just to keep your head on straight. Besides, just like my grandson, you'll pay for your sins soon enough, too. Difference is, you will be a miserable, shitty mess of a man by your *own* hand, where my Tommy boy never stood a chance in hell from the time he was born." She lit another cigarette. "You just *think* about that."

As I turned to walk back to my car, I thought, *Oh, don't worry, lady. I already do, and I imagine I will until the day I die. But sure, why not add a little more insult to injury, right? I'm already a walking corpse.*

And I can see my obituary now: *Ben Striker, local hero cop, found dead from guilt and lung cancer.* Now, there is an epitaph for my kids to be proud of.

#

Actually, I am very lucky I didn't end up being just like Tommy Ray Wallace. My father was the kind of guy you'd picture as a model for an old Norman Rockwell painting, a guy sitting on a porch in an old rocking chair, smoking a corn cob pipe and reading a copy of *National Geographic* or *Arizona Highways*.

But you wouldn't see a faithful old hound dog lying next to the rocking chair, because my father *hated* pets around the house. It had taken me three months to talk him into letting me have a goldfish, and even then he complained about the fish shit odor coming from the tank. But I guess when you slammed down about a case of Pabst Blue Ribbon a day and had the demeanor of an angry pit bull you could always find something to complain about.

But my memories of my Father are the least of my worries these days.

Each morning when I look in my bathroom mirror, it is *Tommy's* face I see, staring back at me accusingly, a ghostly reflection that seems to float right through the misty glass and permeates my very soul.

The only thing that prevents me from cutting my throat is my curiosity about the fragments of memory that bubble to the surface of my mind like turds in a sewer. Some good, some bad. But mostly bad.

That and my family; if it weren't for them, I'd surely have given up by now.

But for now, I'm going to grab a pack of cigarettes, a glass of sun tea, and retire to the back patio and watch the sun go down with my wife, while our beautiful daughters play Frisbee nearby, totally oblivious to my current psychological condition.

Ah...the naive happiness of a child before it is so cruelly ripped away.

Just like the night in the liquor store parking lot, when mine was ripped away as well. I wish my children the best of luck in this world; they are going to need it.

For now, I light a cigarette and sip my tea, as my mind tells me, *It was a righteous kill.*

But my heart screams *murderer.*

Will my heart and mind ever stop pulling me in so many different directions? Maybe, maybe not.

As if my wife can read my mind, she reaches over and grasps my hand gently in her own, gives it a little squeeze, winks at me, and whispers *I love you.*

For now, that's all I really need.

Poor Larry

Larry sat in the front seat of the old Ford pickup, gazing out at the oncoming sunset, welcoming dusk.

It was cooler in the Arizona desert at night, but during the daylight hours, the temperatures were normally in the triple digits, which messed with his gut something awful, since the cancer had set in.

He glanced at his old wristwatch again; almost time for Wild Bill to show up. Bill fancied himself a modern day gunslinger, but in reality, was nothing more than a washed up, alcoholic, former rodeo clown with dellusions of grandeur at best.

But he did make Larry some money on the side now and then, and with the chemo treatments coming up soon, Larry needed the extra scratch.

He heard the sound of Bill's old Chevy in the distance now, spitting and sputtering it;s way through the desert dust at a snail's pace, and appearing to the left of Larry's truck. Bill honked and waved and shut the engine down, then climbed out of the Chevy with an awkward gait, as though already intoxicated this early in the evening.

Larry took a drink himself fairly often these days too, but he has a good reason; for the pain in his guts.

Bill, on the other hand, was just a sloppy, stupid drunk with those...dellusions.

He came staggering up to the passenger's side door of Larry's truck, yanked it open, climbed inside, and said, "Damn...is it *hot* out here."

Larry said, "If you had arrived on time, we'd already be done with business."

Bill reached into his front pocket, retrieved a white envelope full of cash, and laid on the seat next to Larry's leg. He said, "Don't worry, it's all there, as usual."

Larry said, "I had no doubt of that. I was just saying you could have shown up on time for a change."

Bill lit a cigarette and said, "I ran into a problem, no big deal."

Larry said, "You mean you ran into a liquor store, don't you?"

Bill said, "So what? I have a lot on my mind these days."

Larry said, "Of that I have no doubt, either. But one of the most important things you best have on your mind is making us more money. I mean, *big* money for a change, not this nickel and dime bullshit."

Bill said, "It's better than nothing, ain't it?"

Larry's guts suddenly cramped up something awful as he grimaced in pain and said, "You heard what I said, Bill. We need to up the game a bit."

Bill said, "Hurting real bad again, is it?"

"Like sin," Larry said, taking a deep breath. "I ain't never felt anything like it before."

Bill said, "I'm sorry, brother, really I am."

Larry knew that despite Bill's drinking problem, he did have a big heart. He said, "Thanks man, I really appreciate that."

Bill put his cigarette out in the passenger door

ashtray and lit another, and said, "So, I was just thinking, I know this guy."

Rolling his eyes, Larry said, sarcastically, "Let me guess, Pedro, right?"

Bill said, "Yeah, Pedro. What's the problem?"

Larry said, "Because Pedro's brain most likely looks like a piece of fried chicken."

Bill said, "So? He smokes a lot of weed."

Larry said, "That's phrasing it mildly. I bet he'd smoke his own socks if he couldn't score any weed."

Bill said, "Do you want to hear my idea or not?"

Clutching his lower abdomen again, Larry said, "Go ahead, I'm listening."

Bill said, "Yeah, Pedro is an airhead, but he *does* know a lot of street dealers, and *hears* a lot of shit."

Larry said, glumly, "It's the *shit* part I'm worried about."

Bill said, "You wanna hear this or not?"

Larry said, "I said I was listening."

Bill said, "Who do you think it was who set up that last deal for us? The one that made you *a lot* of extra green at the time?"

Larry said, "Yeah, the green that has already been eaten up by my hospital bills."

Bill said, "All the more reason to listen to what I have to say."

Larry said, "Can it wait until tomorrow? I feel like walking death."

Bill said, "Sure, hoss. Tomorrow it is."

As Bill climbed out of the truck, he turned back and said, "Larry?"

Larry said, weakly, "Yeah?"

Bill said, "I'm real sorry about the cancer. I hope

this next plan scores big for you.”

Before Larry could answer, Bill had closed the truck door and was walking away into the oncoming darkness, fading into it like a ghost.

“Thanks, Bill,” Larry said, and started the engine.

#

Once back home, in his tiny, cramped apartment, Larry places the cold vodka bottle against his feverish forehead. Behind his closed eyes, visions of wide-eyed, thrashing bat wings pulse inside his brain from the pain of the cancer that was eating away at his pancreas.

Suddenly, all goes dark behind his eyes; he is engulfed within the blackness as if it is a death shroud. He can see the bones that hold the very earth together, the lonely, cancerous, crumbling bones of lovers past in the vortex of loss.

The loss of his wife.

He still missed her so much, no matter how much she'd hurt his feelings at the time of his diagnosis.

He opened his eyes, leaned against the icebox, and took a big gulp from the bottle. *In sickness and in health*, he thought, glumly. *Til death do us part, my ass.*

He took another drink.

It's the last thing he could remember before hitting the floor.

#

He woke up on the cold linoleum floor a few hours later.

He was cold, dizzy, nauseated, and had a large cigarette burn on his right arm. To add insult to injury, he had also lost control of his bladder during the blackout, and was lying in a pool of his own urine.

Rubbing the sleep fom his eyes and blinking, blinking to clear the images before him, he now sees that, as usual, he was only imagining things, his memory palace so full of cobwebs.

After cleaning himself up, he stumbled into the living room, sat down on the couch, grabbed the bottle of morphine capsules, popped three of them, and chased it with vodka.

He didn't wake up until the next morning, when his cell phone rang.

#

It was Bill.

As Larry reached across the coffee table to retrieve his phone, he almost tumbled into the floor, but righted himself, pushed the talk button, and said, "Do you know what time it is, Bill?"

Bill said, "Around eight am, why?"

Larry coughed, lit a cigarette, and said, "This better be good, Bill."

Bill said, "We better not talk about this over the phone, my friend."

Larry said, "It's really that good?"

Bill said, "Oh yeah."

Larry said, "Be here in twenty."

To Larry's surprise, Bill showed up at his door exactly twenty minutes later.

As they sat down at the small kitchen table, with Larry sipping black coffee and Bill sipping from a small liquor flask, Larry said, "So, what did your genius buddy Pedro come up with?"

Bill said, "It's a great idea, but it comes with some risks."

Larry sipped his coffee, grimaced at the taste, and poured some vodka in it. He said, "What *kind* of risks, pray tell?"

Bill said, "You've heard of that big time drug dealer, Manny Sanchez, right?"

Larry sipped his coffee, poured more vodka in it, and said, "Who hasn't heard of him? He's the only major drug dealer in the county who seems to have the luck of the devil."

Bill grinned and said, "Maybe not for much longer."

Larry said, "Meaning?"

Bill said, "Pedro was at the Conchita Lounge last night, and overheard a conversation between two of Manny's buddies, about a big shipment of both cash, and weed, coming in today."

Larry took a *big* sip of his coffee and said, "I don't think I like where this conversation is going, Billy boy."

Bill said, "It's simple enough; Pedro used to crash at the house where the drugs and cash are going to be stashed, before the city condemned it – and, Manny bought it. He can even draw us a *diagram* of the place, to use when we break in there.”

Larry sat up in his chair and said, “Whoa...Billy boy. Just slow down a bit.”

Bill said, “Just listen to me, give the idea a chance.”

Larry took a big sip of his coffee, and said, “This better be good.”

Bill said, “It's simple, really; we just wait until well after midnight, go through the back basement window to gain access. Then it's up a small flight of stairs to the first floor landing. There are only five rooms. Living room, kitchen, bathroom, and two small bedrooms. I'd imagine they will stash the weed and cash in one of the bedrooms.”

Larry hated to admit it, but it did sound very tempting. He said, “Go on.”

Bill said, “Pedro said he has already checked it out before, and there is only *one* of Manny's bodyguards watching the place at night. That's *it*. We aren't so old and sick we can't take care of *one* greaseball.”

Larry said, “The day I can't take out one greaser is the day I shoot *myself*.”

Grinning, Bill said, “*Exactly*.”

Larry drained his coffee cup, lit a cigarette, and said, “Oh, hell, why not?”

#

The plan was as follows.

That afternoon, Pedro would drop by Larry's place to drop off the diagram – in exchange for a small "donation" to the Pedro weed fund.

Then Larry and Bill would spend the day and early evening studying the diagram, and then, after midnight, the both of them armed with some heavy duty guns and a *I'm here to chew some bubble gum and kick ass* attitude, would take out the guard, sneak into the house under the cover of night, grab the stash, load it into the bed of Larry's truck, and then ride off into the sunset.

That *was* the plan.

But, as with all *perfect* plans, there was always a glitch in there somewhere.

#

By the time Pedro showed up, Larry and Bill were already lit up and loaded for bear.

As Pedro walked into the kitchen, reeking of marijuana and sweat, Larry just kept this mouth shut, thinking about that big score. As Pedro sat down at the table, Larry looked over at Bill and said, "So, *this* is Pedro?"

Before Bill could retort, Pedro said, "Yeah. Who were you expecting? James Bond?"

Larry said, "Why the name Pedro? You are as white as a sheet. Don't look like a greaser to me."

Pedro said, "And you don't exactly look like you're up to this. You *need* me, amigo, so I wouldn't push my luck."

Bill broke into the conversation and said, "Now

now, gentlemen, let's stay focused."

Larry said, "*No*, he hasn't answered my question yet. Pedro?"

Pedro said, "My poppy was white, and my mama was pale skinned Mexican American. Anything else you want to know before we move on?"

Larry sipped his fortified coffee again and said, "No, that'll do for now."

Bill said, "Pedro, show him the diagram."

Pedro reached into his shirt pocket, pulled,out the diagram, unfolded it, and slid it across the table to Larry. He picked it up, glanced over it for a few seconds, and said, "Well, this *looks* simple enough."

Pedro cracked a cocky grin and said, "Yeah, it may *look* simple enough, but it's not."

Larry dropped the diagram on the table and said, "Meaning?"

Pedro said, "*Meaning*, you have to get past the bodyguard first, then, the dog."

Larry reached into the back of his belt and pulled out an old, eight shot, .22 caliber long barrel revolver that had been modified with a silencer. He said, "This little baby fires twenty two magnum, hollowpoint slugs. You ever see what one of these little slugs can do to a man? You go for a headshot, it enters the skull and turns his brains into scrambled eggs."

Bill pulled out an old, Western style, hogleg .40 caliber pistol. He said, "Got this handed down to me from my great, great grandpa. It'll do a number on a man, too, blow him right apart."

Pedro sat back in his chair and said, "Well, that is impressive, but, like I said, you best make sure you get the drop on them *first*, that's all."

Larry said, "You let *us* worry about that. Your job is just to get us *inside*."

Pedro reached into his shirt pocket, pulled out a small, hand rolled, marijuana cigarette, and said, "Fair enough. Now, I suggest we all cop a nice little buzz, and *mellow out* before tonight's festivities."

Larry said, "I *sell* weed, I don't smoke it."

Pedro grinned and said, "You mean, you *steal* it and then sell it, don't you?"

It took all the resolve Larry had to not pick up the .22 and put a bullet in Pedro's forehead, but he managed to do it. He said, "You best watch your mouth, half breed."

Pedro said, "Fair enough. But I still suggest we smoke this joint, mellow out. We go up there all hyped up on booze and morphine, we are the ones who will end up taking the long dirt nap."

Larry really couldn't argue with that. He said, "Fine, then, light it up."

#

By early evening, as mellow as they were liable to be in such a short period of time, they now sat in Larry's truck, about a block away from the stash house, in the dark, watching the body guard from a distance, using a small pair of binoculars Bill had brought along especially for the occasion.

Larry said, "These binoculars are great. Are they military grade?"

Bill said, "Thanks, and yes, military issue. Handed down from my daddy."

Larry said, jokingly, "A long line of military men.

What happened to you?"

Bill said, "I was one of those "make love not war" kind of guys, I guess."

Larry said, "And look at you now."

Pedro pointed at the stash house and said, "Look, fellas."

They all glanced up to see the bodyguard – a tall, massive brute with a buzz cut hair style – walking around outside with the dog.

Lighting a cigarette, Bill said, "Damn...what kind of breed is that?"

Pedro said, "I've seen it up close one day, just walking by. Looks to be a half breed mutt, maybe German Shepard and Pit Bull."

Larry said, "He's a big son of a bitch, that's for sure."

Pedro said, "I'd guess he weighs in at about one hundred pounds, give or take an ounce or two."

Larry said, "Well, he won't do so well against my twenty two magnum."

"Or my hogleg," Bill said, proudly.

Pedro said, "Yeah, well, you'd best go for a headshot, anything other type of wound is just going to piss him off."

Larry said, "You just let *us* worry about that."

Once again, Pedro said, "Guys, look."

They all glanced back toward the stash house to see the bodyguard opening the front door, letting the dog in, and locking it behind him. Then he walked out to the street, climbed into a newer model SUV, and pulled away.

Larry said to Pedro, "Well, mister expert diagram maker, where would you say he's going?"

Pedro said, "Like I said, I've been watching the place, and my guess would be he's on a cigarette run or to the quick stop place around the corner for a big gulp Mountain Dew and a burrito."

Larry *was* impressed. He said, "Damn, Pedro, you have been doing your homework."

Pedro said, proudly, "Damn straight."

Bill said, "Look guys, Godzilla is back already."

They looked up to see the bodyguard was back, and unloading a large bag of dog food from the SUV, carrying it into the stash house, and locking the door behind him again. Then he made a quick call on his cell phone, climbed back into the SUV, and left the house.

Larry said, "Could I be mistaken, or did I just see Godzilla leave for the night?"

Pedro said, "I haven't seen him do that before, but who knows?"

Bill said, "I say we wait for a little while, and if he doesn't come back, we go in, shoot the dog, and grab the stash."

Larry grinned and said, "Sounds like a winner to me."

#

They waited for half an hour, and there was no sign of the bodyguard's return.

Larry said, "I say we go in."

Pedro said, "Not so fast, guys."

Bill said, "Now what?"

Pedro said, "Well, *why* would the bodyguard leave the dog alone in the house, unless he *knew* that the dog could handle the situation all by itself?"

Larry said, "It's a *dog*, Pedro. Nothing more, nothing less."

Bill agreed. He said, "He's right. Ain't *no* dog badass enough to stop bullets."

Larry pushed the driver's side door open, and said, "I'm going in, with or *without* you."

Bill opened the passenger's side door, and said, "Me, too. Coming, Pedro?"

Pedro climbed out of the truck too, but with a *bad* feeling about it all.

#

Once they were through the basement window and up the stairway, they stopped right inside the door that led to the first floor, and listened for the dog.

They heard no paws padding around on the floor, or heavy breathing, no barking, etc. Larry said, "Okay, I'm going to open the door, and when I do, Bill, you go to the left, to the first bedroom, and I'll go right, to the spare bedroom. Pedro, since you are obviously going to be a paranoid pain in the ass, you can just stand in the hallway and act as a look-out. Are we all on board?"

Bill flashed a mock salute and said, "Aye, aye, Captain."

Pedro lit a cigarette and said, "Let's just this over with before I change my mind."

#

As Larry went left and Bill went right, Pedro stood in the hallway, his guts tied up in knots, feeling sick at his stomach.

He was having what he referred to as one of his "paranoid dellusions," often brought on by smoking too *much* weed. *Or*, he thought, *maybe the lack thereof.*

Either way, he wasn't feeling good at all.

Very nervous, actually.

Very...well, *terrified*.

He lit a cigarette, exhaled, and felt a little better, but not much.

Then he heard it.

The faint sound of heavy breathing, then...a deep, guttural, growling sound.

It was very close by.

He looked at the open bathroom doorway across the hall to see it.

The *dog*.

It was so...*huge*, the very sight of it took his breath away – and his ability to speak or scream as well.

But it was too late anyway; it was on him in a split second. It pinned Pedro to the wall with such violent force it knocked the wind completely out of him.

Before Pedro could even regain his balance, the huge beast had already clamped his huge canine teeth down on Pedro's throat, jerking it's huge head back and forth, ripping Pedro's throat wide open, his life blood gushing in an arterial spray with each beat of his terrified heart.

It was over within seconds.

Then the dog was gone, into the darkness, to patiently bide it's time until the other two interlopers showed themselves.

#

Larry had found the money and weed stash in the bedroom and was already bagging it up when Bill walked in, his face as pale as a ghost, shaking so bad he dropped his gun and had to lean down and pick it up.

Larry said, "Damn, brother, are you okay?"

Bill cleared his throat and said, "It's...it's Pedro."

Larry said, "What about him?"

Bill said, "Outside, in the hallway."

Larry dropped the bag, slowly crept over to the doorway, and peeked into the hallway, so see Pedro, his lifeless body slumped against the wall, bleeding out. His dead, lifeless eyes seemed to be *staring* at them, an *accusatory* look, like Pedro was thinking, *Yeah, you guys wouldn't listen, and now look at me. YOU did this to me, you assholes.*

Larry backed up, back into then bedroom, and closed the door. Eyeballing a large chest of drawers close by, he pushed it in front of the door to block it, and said to Bill, "Jeez...that dog almost tore his head off!"

Taking a sip fom his liquor flask, Bill said, "Yeah, and I'd imagine he intends to do the same thing to us."

Larry said, "Well, I'll fist fight that son of a bitch before he stops me from getting out of here with this stash."

Bill said, "Well, since we're trapped in here for now, let's take a look around some more."

Larry said, "First, you try to pry that plywood off of that window, so we can exit through there. I'll take a look around."

While Bill worked on the plywood, Larry checked the nearby closet. As he yanked the sliding doors open, he couldn't believe what he saw.

A large black gym bag, stuffed with more cash. Next to it, another smaller gym bag, stuffed with kilos of cocaine.

He said, "We got here just in time, looks like Manny was getting ready to divide up his ill gotten booty, make some deliveries."

Bill said, "How much, you think?"

Larry said, "With the first stash I found, and now this one, I'd say almost *one million dollars* in cash and drugs."

Bill sipped his flask again and said, "Enough to last us the rest of our lives."

Lighting a cigarette, Larry said, "You betcha, partner."

Bill shined his flashlight on the window and said, "I just hope we get to live long enough to enjoy it."

Larry looked at the window to see the *outside* window frame had been fixed with a set of wrought iron bars. He said, "Well, only one way out now, partner."

Looking at the bedroom door, Bill said, "Hope you're still up for that fist fight, partner."

#

As Larry and Bill divided up their loot into two large bags, making it easier to carry, Bill suddenly whispered, "Did you hear that?"

Larry stopped moving, and breathing; he heard it then, the low breathing – and growling – of the dog, right outside the door.

The *monster* dog.

The dog who killed poor Pedro, who would never enjoy his share of the stash now, after he'd set the whole thing up for them.

Larry quietly leaned over and placed hs head against the door frame, and listened intently, as he heard it *snorting* now, like a bull.

Breathe...snort...breathe...SNORT.

He was beginning to wonder if that damned monster dog from hell might just burst right through that door any second, just like a bull.

Bill whispered, "We ain't going to get out of here alive, are we partner?"

Larry said, glumly, "Well, if we don't, it sure as hell won't be because we didn't try, right, partner?"

Bill said, "Damn straight."

Then suddenly, they heard the sound of it's huge paws moving away from then door, then stopping, then...the dog galloping toward the door, like a bull would gallop toward a rodeo clown.

Then, the sound of the door frame giving way as the huge beast rammed the door with it's head.

Bill said, "Damn! It's trying to bust it's way in here with it's head."

Larry said, "It can't get through there, don't sweat it too much." As quietly as he possibly could, Larry lifted one end of the chest of drawers, moved it aside, leaned down, and peeked through the keyhole.

He could see the massive dog standing about ten feet away from the door, walking around in circles, sniffing and snorting and growling. Then, suddenly, the dog turned to face the door, snorted loudly, and took off in a dead run, smashing into the door with it's massive head.

The door frame came loose again, sending tiny wood splinters flying everywhere. Larry jumped back, pulled his .22 long barrel, aimed it at the door, and fired two shots.

They heard a loud yelping, as at least one of the bullets hit it's mark, and Larry leaned down and looked throuhg the keyhole again, to see one of the slugs had struck the beast in the face, right under it's right eye, and it was running around in a circle again, snarling and growling and going crazy.

Larry said to Bill, "You grab one of of those bags, I'll grab the other, and I'm going to open this door, the both of us blasting away at that dog from hell, then make a run for the basement door."

Bill took a deep breath, picked up the bag, and said, "I'm as ready as I'll ever be, I guess."

Larry picked up the other bag, took a deep breath, and kicked the door open.

The dog immediately turned on them, snarling and growling, as both Larry and Bill ran toward the dog and then past it, Bill firing his gun at the dog as they ran by. The dog began yelping and then snarling again, and caught up to them just as Larry reached the basement door.

Then Larry heard the screaming.

As he turned the basement door knob, he looked back to see the huge beast, with Bill's head in it's jaws, flinging him around the hallway like a rag doll, his skull coming apart.

Larry took one last shot at the beast, but it had no effect. He tried to block the image from his mind as he opened the basement door, ducked inside, and slammed it behind him.

He heard one last, muffled scream as he climbed through the basement window.

#

As soon as he had cleared the window, he was up on his feet, slinging the stash bag over his shoulder and running like the wind around the stash house toward the street, thinking he was home free.

But as he reached the sidewalk, what he saw stopped him dead in his tracks; a traffic cop, standing by his truck, placing a traffic ticket on his windshield.

He did an about face, running back behind the stash house again, eyeballing a line of trees right behind it. He ran past the treeline, huddled up against one of the larger trees, took a deep breath, closed his eyes, and did something he hadn't done since he was a child; he began *praying*.

That's when he heard it.

The blood curdling, gut churning, all too familiar sound of the stash house dog.

He peeked around the tree to see the huge beast had made it through the basement door, out the window, and was now sniffing the air, snorting like a bull, and then fixing it's beady, little evil eyes right on Larry's current location.

Larry turned his head, praying it would go away, when he saw possible salvation up ahead; a small animal shelter hospital, about thirty yards away.

Beggars can't be choosy, he thought, glumly, took another deep breath, and broke into a dead run toward the building.

With the dog hot on his heels.

#

He reached the front door, out of breath and in panic mode, with the dog only about ten yards behind him.

He kicked the door to no avail, then pulled out his .22 magnum and shot the lock mechanism. The door popped open, but with the immediate sound of the building alarm going off, blaring so loud it was almost deafening.

He quickly darted inside, slammed the door behind him, and shot the wall alarm box. It slowly died out, to nothing more than a low humming sound, then ceased altogether.

He glanced out the window to see the dog was just sitting in the parking lot, staring at the buidling. It's face was caked with blood, and it was bleeding profusely from the bullet wounds he and Bill had inflicted upon it.

But it wasn't moving; not one muscle flinch, no barking or growling or snorting.

Just *sitting* there – waiting him out.

He'll bleed out soon, Larry thought, smiling. *Then I'll just stroll right out of here as happy as a fly on a turd.*

He walked over the main office door, nudged it open with his foot, closed the door behind him, sat down at the desk, and lit a cigarette.

As he sat glancing down at the paperwork on the desk, he noticed that there was a list of alarm codes and the electric door lock codes for the cages outside. He'd never seen electric cage doors before, and found it quite interesting.

Then suddenly, his concentration was broken by the sound of the front door being rammed, and the door frame coming apart.

Damn! Larry thought, feeling his guts tighten up. *Why won't this thing DIE?!*

But he received no answer to his inquiry other than another loud *BOOM!* as the beast rammed the door again – and again.

Then it came to him. *If I can lead the dog out to one of those cages, and lock it up inside one of them, I can still get out of here in one piece.*

But...*how?*

Then it came to him again; *the access codes!*

He knew what he was going to do now.

He would climb out of the office window, flank to the left, and run as fast as he could to one of the cages, using the access codes to enter it, and try to lure the dog into one of them, and trap him there.

That's when noticed that the door slamming had stopped.

He peeked out the front office window to see the dog was sitting about twenty feet from the front door, weaving back and forth on it's paws, weak from blood loss, it's face battered and broken.

But Larry wasn't going to take any chances.

He grabbed the stash bag, slung it over his shoulder, grabbed the access codes, stuffed them into his shirt pocket, opened the office window, and gently lowered himself to the ground outside.

So far, so good.

#

He slowly crept around the side of the building, keeping within the shadows, and peeked around the edge of the building to see the dog was still sitting there, weaving back and forth, it's beady eyes fixed on the front door.

Larry took another deep breath, exhaled, said a silent prayer, and took off in a dead run toward the cages.

That's when he heard the dog's huge bloody paws pounding the pavement behind him.

He didn't bother looking back.

The dog was gaining on Larry fast, it's huge paws spattering the concrete with bloody paw prints, it's huge maw open, the razor sharp teeth gnashing up and down like it was nothing more than a maniacal eating machine.

Larry wheeled around in mid-stride, fired off another shot, and wheeled back around just in time to jump into a large dog cage, slam the door shut behind him, and cower down in one corner of the cage, the .22 already cocked again and ready for battle.

With that, the huge beast began slip-sliding on the pavement until it came to a dead stop with it's bloody forehead slamming into the cage like a cruise missle, almost caving the door in from the outside.

The beast stepped back, shaking it's head to clear it, and sat staring at Larry, it's massive chest heaving and it's hot, foul breath almost choking Larry from six feet away.

He leaned back to catch his breath again, regain some composure. It was at that moment he realized that he hadn't heard one sound coming from the other outside dog cages. He glanced around to see that some of the cages had broken into, and now contained nothing more than the ruined carcasses of the dogs, the blood pooling in front of the cages and appearing almost black in the moonlight.

Crazy son of a bitch, Larry thought in anger. *It kills anything it can get's it paws on. But it won't kill ME.*

The other dogs that were still alive were all cowered in the corner of their cage – just like he was – and not making a sound, in fear of the beast's wrath being inflicted upon them as well.

He looked away, shook his own head to clear it, and checked his gun.

Only three shots left, and no extra ammo.

At least not enough to kill it, anyway. *Maybe if I had a bazooka? Or a hand grenade?*

But all he had was a dog whistle he'd found on the desk, a gun with three bullets, and what was left of his wits.

He glanced back up at the beast.

It was still staring at him.

Waiting for just the right moment, so quietly and patiently.

#

To his utter astonishment, Larry had nodded off.

He awoke with a start, his eyes searching the semi-darkness for any signs of the beast.

He saw the dog had entered the cage right next to him, and was lying on it's stomach, it's evil, red hot eyes still fixed on him, waiting patiently for it's opportunity to take him apart limb from limb.

Larry sat motionless, conserving every last ounce of strength he had left. He lit his next to the last cigarette, blew smoke in the beast's direction, just to be an asshole. The dog bared it's bloody teeth and growled.

"Bite me," Larry said, jokingly. "Bite my skinny little hairy ass."

That's when it happened.

With a loud humming sound, the auxiliary power to the property came on.

The cage door lock on the big dog's cage automatically *locked*.

So did Larry's cage door, but he had the *manual access code*.

With big grin on his face, Larry stood up, brushed himself off, and said, "Checkmate, you big evil bastard. I *gotcha*."

Larry typed in the code on his box and the door buzzed open. He walked out, stood about ten feet from the beast's cage, and smiled. "Bite me," he said once again, turned around, and pulled down his pants. "Bite me, bite me, *bite* me!"

The beast looked at the door lock on it's own cage, and began growling and snarling again. Larry took the dog whistle from his pocket, placed it in his mouth, and blew into it as hard as he could.

The beast went bonkers again, this time worse that Larry had ever seen him act before. He began ramming the cage door with it's head again, over and over, the hinges coming loose and blood from the beast's wounds spattering the cage floor.

Larry knew he didn't have much time.

He blew into the dog whistle again, as hard as he could, and at the same time, cocked the hammer back on the .22.

Aimed it right at the beast's head.

As the beast rammed the cage door again, Larry pulled the trigger.

He *missed*.

SHIT! He thought, blowing on the dog whistle again. The dog went ballistic, yelping in pain and frustration and snapping it's teeth and ramming the door again. He cocked the hammer back again, and fired.

The bullet struck the cage door panel, destroying the lock mechanism and and sending red hot sparks flying through the air, some of them landing on the beast's face, and he howled in pain, and readied himself for another charge at the door.

Larry had *one* bullet left.

As the dog charged the door again, Larry leveled the gun right at the dog's head again, and pulled the trigger.

The bullet struck the beast in the forehead, and it slammed into the burning door box panel head-first, sending even more sparks flying through the air. There was a hot, sizzling sound, like bacon frying, as the beast's head exploded in a haze of tiny flames. The beast yepled and howled one last time, and fell to the ground in a bloody, burnt heap, it's entire body convulsing for a few moments, then it lay still.

The acrid stench from the smoking fur and burning flesh was overpowering, and Larry had to cover his mouth and nose and step back.

It was at that moment that his mind and body, having taken all the mental and physical abuse they could for one night, shut down.

He stumbled awkwardly on his feet, falling

backward and landing hard on his butt, the concrete wet and unforgiving underneath him. He winced at the pain, tears streaming from his eyes, as he fumbled to light his last cigarette.

The cigarette was broken.

He laughed out loud – sort of a maniacal laugh.

Then he just sat there and stared at the burning, smoldering mess for the longest time.

Thinking about his past, and how lucky he was to still be alive – although his guts were starting to cramp with pain again, and he didn't have any of his morphine capsules handy.

He was still sitting there when heard the sound of police sirens in the distance, and saw flashing lights out of the corner of his eye.

Under the circumstances, he couldn't help but laugh at that, too.

A few moments later, he was past the treeline, and on his way back home; he had a parking ticket to take care of before his vacation.

Sara Has A Monkey On Her Back

When Sara comes home at the end of the day there is no one there waiting for her.

She switches on the bare bulb that hangs in the kitchenette. Her hands are sweating and smell like smoke, fast food, and coffee. The police uniform she'd put on just eight hours ago now hangs limply from her exhausted frame. She blinks her heavily made up eyes as she grabs a bottle of vodka from the ancient icebox.

She takes a large swallow, grimaces as the cheap booze burns it's way down her throat as it lands in her stomach like a lead balloon, exploding into hundreds of tiny little fireballs as it careens into her bloodstream.

Then...*euphoria.*
Salvation.

She places the cold bottle against her feverish forehead. Behind closed eyes, visions of wide-eyed, thrashing bat wings pulse inside her brain.

Then, darkness.

#

As usual, when she awakens from the self medication, she is alone again.

She glances around the room, her bleary eyes fixed on what she is sure the shadow of her long lost love, but, once again, it is merely the shadows of the neon lights from the bar across the street shining through her window, and turning her sparse furnishings into dark, spectral beasts; her bed a tomb, her closet a dark abyss into another world, her bedside stand a shrine to a chain smoker.

Rubbing the sleep fom her eyes and blinking, blinking to clear the images before her, she now sees that, as usual, she was only imagining things, her memory palace so full of cobwebs.

She rises from the old tattered bed and peeks out of the window at the street below. *It's really funny*, she thinks, *how the people down below, on the street, look like a bunch of bugs scampering madly about, on their way to hell knows what and don't even care, really, as long as they feel better – if only briefly.*

Just like me.

She suddenly realized she wanted to feel better too, if only for a short period of time, and, in someone's arms, even if it is a stranger.

But she decides to stay home again instead.

Misery loves company.

#

Sara has the next day off so she decides to clean her service weapon.

Glancing around, she notices that she needs to clean house too, but, currently suffering from a crippling vodka hangover, she opts to sit at the kitchen table and clean her gun instead.

Staggering slightly as she made her way to the kitchen, she unzipped her jeans and dropped them to the floor of the living room, then half-naked, returned to the kitchen, where she picked up her gun case and retrieved her tools of the trade; bristle brush, bore rod, and oily rag. She picks up the gun to clean it and her hands are shaking so bad she drops it on the floor, almost landing on her foot.

She knows this isn't going to cut it so she opens the fresh bottle of vodka sitting on the table and pours three fingers into an old jelly jar and sips slowly at first, then faster as she realizes slow-sipping isn't going to cut it, either.

By the time half of the bottle is gone, she is ready to clean the gun. Or she thought she was.

Realizing now that she is getting a little too buzzed to clean her gun properly, she now opts for the house cleaning idea instead. By the time she has washed a few dishes and swept the floor, she is out of breath, so she sits down for a cigarette break.

And another three fingers of vodka.

#

She woke up on the cold linoleum floor a few hours later.

She is cold, dizzy, nauseated, and has a large cigarette burn on her right thigh.

She finally manages to get up off the floor, her head filled with visions of her past, flashing through her mind like a VHS tape on fast-forward. She sees her parents – both now deceased – in a happier time, both much younger and full of life. She sees her dog, Toby, her childhood pet, scampering to meet her as she exits the school bus. He was struck by a car when she was nine years old, leaving her heartbroken for months. She felt so alone after his death, being an only child.

She sees her father – also a police officer - sitting at the kitchen table, nursing a hangover with a can of beer, while her mother stands close by washing the dishes and avoiding any conversation with him. She knew better than to voice her opinion to an ill tempered, foul mouth drunk, so she opted to stay silent as opposed to being subjected to another beating.

She closed her eyes and the visions began all over again, like a long lost friend. As quickly as the visions had begun, they cease altogether. Marla feels dizzy again. She staggers into the kitchen and retrieves the last bottle of vodka from the top cabinet and sits back down at the table, pops the cap, takes a drink, and lights a cigarette. Just to take the edge off, you know. A little hair of the dog that bit her never hurts, right? Just this one time.

After several more drinks and another cigarette, she decides to take a shower.

After she has another drink.

#

And so it goes.

She is slowly but surely ending up just like her father; a career cop with a monkey on her back and a bad attitude who is slowly but surely coming apart at the seams.

And then there was Todd, the son of a bitch.

Her fiance, Todd, had recently broken up with her, without even as much as a Dear John letter, a phone call, a hi or bye or kiss my ass, either.

He hadn't even had the decency to break it off in person. He broke up with Sara by email. Chickenshit.

But he had told her that "it isn't you, it's me," by way of a half-ass explanation. Just some more BS and drama he'd most likely picked up from Facebook. In a way she was glad. In a way she was miserable, too. She still loved him but hated him too. Same old shit, just different day for a female rookie cop more or less "married to her job."

As good excuse as any, she guessed.

Maybe she *was* married to her job.

Or, better yet, *trapped* in it, with no way out – except for a bottle of cheap vodka.

She guessed she'd find out soon enough.

#

After the floor mopping and washing a small load of laundry, Sara finally felt strong enough to cook something to eat.

Or, *microwave* something to eat, that is.

She looked into the small freezer to see she was in dire need of taking a walk to the corner market, too.

After a cigarette break - and a small shot of vodka – off she went.

#

She was all too familiar with the corner market.

Her first day on the job – her very first *call* on the job – was at this market.

She was on top of the world that day; she'd graduated the police academy, got her own apartment {goodbye miserable dysfunctional home life!} and had spent her first night there, sleeping like a baby on her new water-bed.

The next day, she and her riding partner, Abe Moss, had received their first call of the day; armed robbery in progress at the corner market.

A neighbor had called in on numerous occasions complaining about all the racket coming from next door, coming from the market. Sounded like screaming and gunshots.

They arrived at the scene to find the front door broken off the hinges – and blood spatter visible on the wall behind the front counter. She drew her service weapon, announced herself, and with no response, slowly crept inside, with Abe right behind her.

There was nobody there – at least not alive. Lying on the blood stained carpet behind the counter was a young woman close to her own age. Gunshot wound to the right side of her face. After she radioed in for back up, Sara stepped closer to see the young woman was partially naked, her clothing ripped and torn and in total disarray.

Her left ring finger was missing, most likely severed with a pair of pruning shears. No doubt her killer wanted her gold wedding band and it was hard to slip off so they'd chose to remove the ring in a much less conventional fashion.

Sara ran outside to throw up, leaving Abe inside alone, waiting for the backup.

It was after that she'd started drinking too much after work. Just to take the edge off, you know.

It was not too long after that Todd had become distant, stopped coming by as often, and had eventually ended the relationship by email. Marla had called him a chickenshit. She realized now that he was only looking out for his best interests, hadn't relished the idea of watching her drink herself to death.

It was also after that Sara had realized that her father was a good man long ago and far away, until he allowed the job to get him down. Instead of coming home and talking about his day, he kept it bottled up inside, doing what he thought was best for his family, protecting them from the horrors of the real world, the horrors of being a homicide detective – but trying to escape the horrors with alcohol.

And so it goes.

#

As she strolled through the market, grabbing the obligatory bachelorette snacks – microwave sandwiches, TV dinners, Ramen noodles, and Pringles chips – she felt a sudden sense of claustrophobia, like the walls were closing in on her.

The feeling was almost overwhelming this time, and she had to stop by the beer cooler in back, take several deep breaths, trying to regain her composure. After a few moments she took one last deep breath, exhaled, and walked up to the checkout line.

The owner – the father of the girl killed there long ago – didn't even recognize her.

#

On her way home, she suddenly felt dizzy, almost tripping over her own feet.

She stopped again, leaned against a light pole, closed her eyes, and began taking deep breaths again to clear her head. Then she walked on again, praying silently to get home without losing her shit out in a public place.

That monkey on her back was waking up again, and he was *thirsty*.

She knew the feeling.

#

Afterf a dinner of Ramen noodles, Ritz crackers, and spring water, it's time for a beer.

It isn't quite cold yet, kind of lukewarm, actually, but she doesn't really care because it's making her hands shake less – and it isn't the demon vodka – that monkey that's always riding her backside like a long lost lover.

After two lukewarm beers and an ice cold beer, she realizes beer isn't going to cut it after all, and sits staring at the icebox like she's in a trance, doing her best to stay seated, because she knows that *monkey* is in the freezer.

Her hands are clammy and beads of sweat break out on her forehead and her stomach suddenly threatens to toss up her dinner if she doesn't give in to the monkey.

She begins to cry, quietly at first, then the tears fall like rain and she sobs so loudly, making a sound like she, herself, has never heard before, even from the family members of murder victims. A loud wailing like a wounded animal, caught in a trap, with no way out.

She feels like total shit; like a five foot, four inch, one hundred and twenty pound pile of human waste.

That's what she felt like at that very moment; a piece of human waste, no better than the walking wounded she had to place under arrest on a daily basis.

It seemed like she cried forever.

When her tears finally ran dry and she had tossed up her dinner and had taken a long hot shower, she opened her bedroom window, turned on her floor fan, and laid down for what would be, at best, a very fitful night's sleep.

She knew that, regardless of how she felt in the morning, she had to go to work, pay a visit to Sergeant

Striker's office, and tell him the truth.

She had to come *clean* – in every sense of the word – and move forward with her life as best she could, but *sober* this time.

If her honesty cost her her job as a police officer, so be it; at least she was honest about it, and did the right thing. She would rather fry burgers at a fast food joint for the rest of her life than allow the monkey on her back to interfere with her job performance – and God forbid, possibly get her partner or an innocent civilian killed in the process.

As she closed her eyes that night, she was hoping that her Sergeant would understand, give her a second chance.

Her sleep was fitful at best.

#

The next day, after donning her not so crisp uniform and making it to the precinct just in the nick of time for roll call, Sara was more than just a little worse for wear.

She pulled through, though, and, before meeting up with Abe at the parking lot, dropped by Sergeant Striker's office to have a short but so sweet chat about her "problem."

She had always been more than just a little intimidated by Striker; at six feet, four inches tall and weighing in at around two forty, with his bulging biceps and broad shoulders and a face that looked like it had been carved out of granite, it was hard not to feel a little nervous around him at first glance.

As she stopped at his office door and knocked, she could feel her stomach begin to lurch again like it had the night before, and had to fight with all of her being not to vomit as a deep, gruff voice coming from inside the office said, "Come in."

Taking a deep breath, she walked in to see Striker sitting at his desk drinking coffee. He said, "Officer Sara Walker. I hope this is important, I haven't even finished my first cup of coffee yet."

He said it in a joking fashion, with his trademark "half-ass" smile, but she didn't want to take any chances. She said, apologetically, "I'm sorry, sir. Should I come back later?"

Looking her over like a scientist would examine a lab rat, he said, "It's fine. Have a seat."

She sat down, crossing her legs and folding her hands in her lap. She said, nervously, "I have something to tell you that I believe you should know."

Looking her over again, he said, "Don't bother. I know a bad hangover when I see one. It's in the eyes, the pallor of your skin, the shaky hands. You're getting ready to take the walk of shame, and you're so nervous that you feel like you could throw up. Am I correct in my assumption?"

"The walk of shame?" Sara said, her stomach tied up in knots.

He said, "Yes, the walk of shame. The walk you're getting ready to take when you leave my office."

Swallowing a lump in her throat, she said, "Sir?"

He said, "Don't worry, you're not fired – although you should be. But, God knows, if I had always fired a good cop for having a monkey on their back, half of my department would be flipping burgers at Wendy's."

She said, "So...where do we go from here, sir?"

He sipped his coffee, stood up, and said, "It's

where *you* go from here, officer Walker. First of all, I'm placing you on a one month suspension, without pay for the first two weeks. You will also see the department shrink during this time period, as well as attending AA meetings indefinitely. At the end of your suspension, if I feel as though you still have a monkey on your back, you will take the walk of shame for the *last* time. Are we clear on this matter?"

Wringing her hands nervously, Sara said, "Yes, sir. As clear as a bell, sir."

Striker held out his right hand and said, "Your badge and gun, officer Walker."

She handed them over and said, "Sir?"

He said, "Yes, officer Walker?"

She said, "Why are you giving me a break? I mean, honestly?"

He sat back down, sipped his lukewarm coffee, opened the top drawer of his desk, and pulled out her personnel file, and laid it on the desk. He said, "Because, officer Walker, I have been keeping tabs on you for a while now. I know all about your personal background, education, and family history. And what I see is a *good* cop – with the potential to be a *great* cop – if she just gets her shit wired tight."

She said, "Is that the *only* reason, sir?"

He said, "Meaning?"

She said, "Is it because I am a woman?"

He said, "Just between you and me? I have been in your shoes too, early in my career. Somebody gave me a second chance, too. But that's our little secret, right?"

Cracking a grin, she said, "Just between you and me, sir, yes."

He said, "Fine, then. Now, go get your shit together, officer Walker."

Blinking away tears, she stood at attention, saluted him,, and said, "Yes, sir. Getting my shit together, sir."

Then she took the walk of shame – but with her head held high.

#

Twenty-eight days later, Sara Walker walked into Sergeant Striker's office, with her head still held high, sober for twenty-six of those days.

When she walked in, Striker was sitting at his desk as usual, sipping his morning coffee, looking over Sara's personnel file on his desktop. Upon looking up to see Sara standing there, bright eyed and bushy tailed, he smiled and said, "So, I see you got my phone message."

She sat down and said, "Yes, sir. But it hasn't been thirty days, yet, sir."

He said, "I know, but I have been keeping up with your progress, and I must admit, you've done remarkably well."

She said, "Thank you sir. I feel a lot better."

He said, "I bet you do." He opened his top desk drawer and retrieevd something he had hidden in the palm of his hand, and said, "That's why I'm giving you a promotion."

Before she could reply, he placed the palm of his hand on the desk top and slid two small cloth patches across th desk toward her. When he removed his hand, there was a pair of Corporal stripes.

She said, "Sir?"

He said, "Congratulations, Corporal Walker. You've come a long way."

Fighting back tears, she said, "I don't understand, sir."

He said, "I'm giving you a promotion for your efforts, Sara. You've fought a battle over the last few weeks – and *won* that battle – that a lot of people can't win in a lifetime."

She said, "To be honest, sir, I don't know if I can do this."

In an angry tone, he said, "That's BS, and you know it. Look at what you've been through in your life, and you've come through it all, smelling like a rose. Now, stop this nonsense, get your shit wired tight, and be here first thing in the morning, Corporal Walker, to start your new shift." He retrieved her badge and gun from his top drawer, and placed them on the desk top as well. "Are we clear on this situation?"

"Yes, sir," she said, picking up the badge, gun, and stripes. "First thing in the morning, sir."

As she turned to walk out, Striker said, "And Corporal?"

She turned around and said, "Yes, sir?"

He said, "Make me – and your Father – proud, Corporal Walker."

Saluting him, she said, "I will, sir, I promise."

Then she was walking down the hall, her head still held high, on her way to a new life.

As she walked out into the parking lot, into the beautiful summer weather, she stopped, glanced up at the sky, closed her eyes, and thought, *And thank you, too, Daddy, for making me so tough, just like you.*

Jack and Norma Jean

Fall, 1963, Dallas, Texas

Around nine a.m. on the twenty first, I heard a knock at my door. I picked up my Russian made handgun from the nightstand and cocked it. I would normally receive phone calls from my clients as opposed to personal visits, so I had to be careful. In my line of work, you had to have eyes in the back of your head. I walked to the door, the gun ready, adrenaline pumping.

"Yeah?" I said, placing the end of the barrel against the peephole.

"It's Ivan," a deep voice told me. Old Ivan was frightening, he was. A big Ruskie, too. I opened the door. "Howdy, Ivan," I said. He just glared at me and walked on by. Me and Ivan sat down at my small table, and he pulled a large manila envelope out of his jacket and laid it on the table and scooted it over to me.

"Open it," he said, with a steely glare. I picked it up and slit the end of it open with my hunting knife and let the contents spill out onto the table top. There was the usual, obligatory paperwork, along with a stack of black and whites. I picked one of the photos up and glanced at it, to see a man in a dark suit wearing a big smile and waving to an adoring crowd. Could he be a movie star? I thought. I asked Ivan who it was.

"That's the target," he said, nonchalantly.

"Handsome devil," I said, lighting a smoke. "Popular with the ladies, is he?"

"You've heard of Marilyn Monroe?" He asked, giving me a big, shit eating grin as he lit up a Cuban cigar. Ivan thought those cigars smelled like class. To me, they smelled like shit.

"No shit?" I said.

"No shit, comrade." He said.

As we sat and smoked Cuban cigars and drank cheap beer, talking about the plans, Ivan reached down and grabbed a briefcase he'd brought in with him, laid it on the table. "Open it," he said. I opened it to find the whole eight hundred grand, in hundreds, fifties, and twenties.

"All of it now, huh?"

"Yes," Ivan said. "We'd prefer it if you'd disappear right after it's done. You wouldn't have time to collect it afterward."

"Too risky?" I inquired.

"You heard what I said," he replied.

"No problem, comrade."

"Make sure there isn't," he said, then got up from his seat and walked out the door without another word. Ivan was like that; all business.

I walked over to my closet, pulled out my rifle. She was old, but I kept her clean, in good shape. After I cleaned her up, I sat down with a can of Red Rocket beer to watch TV. There was a film clip playing of Marilyn Monroe singing happy birthday to the President.

Man...she was *hot*.

I didn't know why then, but I sat there debating on whether or not to take the money and run.

#

Then there was the wooden fence on the grassy knoll.

The Warren Commission findings and the single bullet theory are all implausible to some researchers. Oswald's rifle, through testing by the FBI, could be fired – even by an inexperienced shooter – three times within less than eight seconds. Through so called "eye witnesses" it was determined that *three* bullets were fired; one hit Kennedy and passed through governor Connelly's arm, the second one went astray, and the third slammed into Kennedy's head, knocking it backward. There is also the "magic bullet" theory, in which there were two shooters, and the second shooter's single bullet was the one that killed him.

There were also too many eye witness testimonies to put together any plausible theories at all, some of which were the bullets came from the grassy knoll, they came from the depository, they came from a moving vehicle on the nearby overpass, which means there would have been two shooters, because the bullets trajectory would have been from the front *and* the back.

Then there was the "three tramps" theory, in which three different vagrants were questioned that day because of their close proximity to the crime at the moment of the shooting. One of the tramps, Charles Harrelson, father of actor Woody Harrelson, boasted about his involvement at the time – just for the publicity and a free meal – but later, in a 1988 interview, he denied even being near Dallas at the time of the shootings.

I look back on it now and can't help but wonder; were there really two of us that day? What connection did Marilyn Monroe have – if any – to the assassination? Was she in on it? Did she feel spurned by him for not leaving his wife for her, and paid someone to kill him?

In order to understand what exactly did or did not happen in the last few years leading up to her death, and why, it's important to take a better examination of the facts.

Take for example the night she sang happy birthday to the President. As she'd begun to sing, she'd seemed suddenly energized, perhaps from the Dexedrine pills that had been prescribed by her personal physician. Combined with huge doses of megavitamins and antibiotics, it was a like a mass seduction, with all the men present under her spell and yelling and screaming for more. Was her addiction to certain types of drugs a big factor in her judgment being clouded when it came to her and JFK's affair?

So many questions and so few real answers.

Only speculations.

On one occasion – according to certain "insiders," JFK and Marilyn had been spending a lot of time together in a small apartment connected to a tunnel that led to the Carlyle Hotel, where JFK maintained a penthouse. But what had kept them locked up inside the apartment that particular day wasn't sex, because she had complained to him he was "perfunctory" in bed, and "made love like an adolescent."

They'd also been known to spend hours on end talking on the phone to each other, gossiping about private Whitehouse affairs, which of course was none of her business, and a definite threat to the nation's security, considering her frame of mind and penchant for gabbing about anything that happened to enter her mind at any given moment.

Then there was the Jack Ruby conspiracy theory, too.

#

November 21st, 1963

I got tired of watching *Rawhide* reruns, so I decided to take a walk down to O'Reilly's bar for a drink. I could only take so much boredom in those days, between jobs. Afterward, I walked down to a men's clothing shop, an *expensive* shop, and treated myself to a new outfit.

I bought a leather flight jacket, corduroy pants, and red, snakeskin boots.

The price tag was over a grand, but what else did I have to spend my money on, right? I already had a tidy little nest-egg hidden away for a rainy day, and after this job, I'd never have to worry about anything again. After leaving the clothing shop, looking like a new man, I'd decided to go back to O'Reilly's for one more drink. I met a blond there, believe it or not, that looked just like Marilyn Monroe. Talk about irony.

#

The blonde and I had ended up going back to my room, {she told me she loved "macho" guys in black leather}, taken a roll in the hay, then she'd left, fifty dollars richer. I didn't usually go out with hookers, but I couldn't pass up the chance to sleep with one that looked like Marilyn Monroe. I look back now, and I think part of it was an ego trip, too. Men are predictable, as much as I hate to admit it. I had the new threads and the green, so I took advantage of it. Hell....who wouldn't?

After she'd left, {for some odd reason, I'd felt an overwhelming sense of loss}, I'd sat back down to watch some more TV and relax. There was more news about the president on TV, and his visit to our fair city the next day. Even on the TV screen, he had a strong presence, I'll have to admit, and a real flair for the dramatic, too. A real good talker, and I was sure his looks didn't hurt as far as getting votes, either. One guy, a younger fella who sort of resembled the President, called him "Jack." But, then, I'd hear someone refer to him as John. To me, though, he looked like a Jack. I even detected some sort of accent in his speech, like rural Maine or some shit.

This guy was dangerous to the United States? I'd thought maybe Ivan had brought me the wrong file. A danger to the ladies, maybe, or their husbands, but that was about it as far as I could see. Then again, I'd never had a high IQ.

Then again, although I wasn't the sharpest quill on the porcupine, I wasn't the dullest, either.

I had begun to wonder what kind of personal life he had; wife, kids, mistress? As far as TV appearances are concerned, I knew looks could be deceiving. Still, it was hard for me to believe a man with this much going for him, this much charisma, would be dead soon. I popped another beer.

#

Many take it for granted that if there was an assassination conspiracy, Jack Ruby must have been involved. In fact, many people believe there was a conspiracy precisely because of Ruby's murder of Lee Harvey Oswald, which had the effect -- intentional or not -- of silencing the accused assassin.

But whether there was a conspiracy or not, there is no reason to assume that Ruby must have been involved. In fact, logic tells us that no conspiracy could profit by silencing Oswald in a public fashion: What's the point of eliminating one suspect while simultaneously handing the police another? Also, was it Oswald's intention to "talk," he'd already had nearly 48 hours in which to do so. Every minute he waited only diminished the chance that others involved could be apprehended. By that time, any conspirators would have to assume he'd already spilled his guts.

Another factor to be considered is whether Ruby was the type of person to be entrusted with any responsibility, when a single word from him could have resulted in the arrest of others involved. Dallas reporter Tony Zoppi knew Ruby well and says one "would have to be crazy" to entrust Ruby with anything important, that he "couldn't keep a secret for five minutes. Jack was one of the most talkative guys you would ever meet. He'd be the worst fellow in the world to be part of a conspiracy, because he just plain talked too much. Jack Ruby would be the last one that I could ever trust to do anything," said Ruby's rabbi, Hillel Silverman.

I couldn't have said it better myself.

#

November 22nd, 1963
9:30 A.M.

I woke up early on the 22nd. I had showered and shaved by 9 a.m. I would spend the next three hours sitting in an old tattered chair in front of my motel room window, watching the world below me go by. The old sign outside my window had two bulbs burnt out, so it was flashing DE ROP INN in red and blue. Any other time, I'd found it amusing, but I was trying to stay in a serious frame of mind that day, had important business to attend to.

I sat there in my low key, low profile room, a high powered rifle resting on my lap, still debating on going through with the business at hand. I felt as though I'd been lying to myself for the last thirty-six hours; I didn't really want this job. The money, yes. The job, no.

It was a hard line to draw in my line of work; separating the wants from the want - nots. I had a suitcase filled with $799,090 sitting on my bed, new clothes, and a new identity, if I wanted one.

I had a chance to run away from my life as I'd known it and never look back.

But, if I chose to do so, I knew I'd be looking over my shoulder the rest of my natural life, however long that might be or not be. My present clients weren't the kind to be trifled with. I sat in that chair for two hours, fifty one minutes. Then I got up, took a deep breath, let it out, then grabbed my rifle and suitcase and walked out the door to my destiny.

#

On his death bed, Jack Ruby had said he couldn't remember doing any of it. Grant you, he may have been under the influence of pain relieving drugs and such, but still, for a guy who'd been hell-bent on so much fame and publicity, you think he'd remember at least a little about the day he shot the guy who'd killed JFK. Or thought he had, anyway.

Wait…I'm not only getting ahead of myself again, but possibly boring those of you not familiar with this information as well. Allow me to go back to the time when I'd met the blonde in O'Reilly's bar. She is actually the pivotal character in this little drama, so I'll go back to her for now.

Thirty years later – as I'd sat on my own private little stretch of beach in the Caymans – soaking up rum and watching the half naked ladies stroll by, I'd suddenly spotted a woman that looked very familiar to me coming up the beach.

Even from a distance, I knew who she was; the same Marilyn Monroe look-alike I'd met in O'Reilly's bar all those years ago. As I watched her coming up the beach, I was suddenly reminded of that old Bo Derek film, *10*, where she is running up the beach in slow motion, her long braided hair blowing in the ocean breeze. The blonde looked that way to me at that moment – at least in my mind's eye, anyway – her long blonde hair blowing back from her face, revealing the fact she hadn't seemed to have aged a day in all those years.

She was wearing a lime green sundress, open toed sandals, and had a big carry-all bag slung over one shoulder, like she'd packed an overnight bag just in case she happened to find me there. I had started to feel as though I was stuck in the middle of an old *Twilight Zone* episode. By the time she'd reached the front stoop of my little love shack, my fantasy was over, and I'd come back to reality, although I'd fought hard not to. My dreams and fantasies were often times the only places I felt safe.

"Fancy meeting you here," she said, slipping off her sandals and placing that shapely derriere down on my bottom step. She looked tired and sort of anxious, as though she'd come a long way to find me and hoped she wouldn't be disappointed.

"You stole my opening line," I said, swinging my legs off of the deluxe chaise lounge chair that was now drenched in sweat and tan oil. "That's not good for a man's ego, you know."

"Sorry," she said, sifting the sand with her toes. Her toenails were polished the same color as her sundress and peppered with glitter. *Sexy.* "Want me to walk back down the beach, start all over again?"

I waved it off. "Not necessary. Don't want to ruin the moment. Speaking of the moment, how...*why* did you find me?"

"In all honesty, it was just by chance, really, a coincidence."

"That's putting it mildly. How did you recognize me after all these years?"

"You haven't changed all that much, really. You

are actually more handsome now than you were back then."

"And you are just as beautiful," I said, meaning it, too. Mother Nature and Father Time had been very kind to her. "Are you thirsty? I just made a pitcher of Long Island ice tea."

"I'd love a glass, I'm parched."

I poured her a glass and she sat down next to me, sipping her drink and gazing out at the gorgeous sunset in silence for a moment, then, "Surely you know why I'm *really* here, don't you?" she said, looking deep into my bloodshot eyes.

Then I knew; all of the pieces fit together now, like a puzzle. She had been at O'Reilly's bar for a *reason*, a reason that was all too terrifyingly clear to me now. I cleared my throat and said, "So, how much did they pay you to sleep with me? It must have been a lot more than I paid you."

She smiled at that. "Does it really matter now?"

"I guess not," I said, glumly.

"So, shall we get on with this? I have a plane to catch."

"Do I get a ten second head start for old time's sake?" I asked, hoping she'd go for it, considering my age.

"Sorry, you know the rules," she said, reaching into her oversized purse.

"Yeah, unfortunately, I do," I said, and grabbing her by the arm before she had a chance to clear her purse with the .25 automatic. I was twisting hard, her face a mask of pain and fear as I slowly but surely wrestled her to the sand and pressed the barrel against her chin. She gave me that puppy dog look little kids give you when they know they have a royal ass-whipping coming and don't want one.

"Sorry," I said, as I slowly squeezed the trigger. "You know the rules."

#

Here is my general outlook on life; the world is full of broken people, lonely people, and hungry people. It's part of the natural order of things. But, splints, casts, so called miracle drugs, or even time itself, can't mend broken hearts, wounded minds, or spirits torn asunder, let alone a perpetually empty belly.

Or the fact I'm slowly but surely dying of cancer. You would have thought I'd welcomed a much quicker and less painless death at the hands of the blonde with the .25, but you'd be wrong.

As Charlie Chaplin once said, "In the end, everything is just a gag." He apparently was an optimist by nature. Me?

Not so. I'd always had a lot of trouble finding a silver lining in every cloud, or a pot of gold at the end of every rainbow. In other words, I may have *read* fiction, or *watched* it on the screen, but, I didn't *live it.* I tried my best to remain in a virtual state of reality, no matter how hard times were to deal with.

It all seems like a life time ago now.

Then again, when you've spent half of your life chasing ghosts, you tend to lose track of time in the sense that most of us experience it. That, along with having been a career alcoholic and pill popper, tends to cloud a person's mind just a tad bit after so many lost years go by like a blur.

The heroin is taking care of the pain most of the time, but I'm still having trouble with my personal hygiene and feeding myself.

And through it all, through the cloud of pain and the sleepless nights and the bad dreams and the fact I know I'm going to be dead soon, that one, burning question still lingers in the back of my mind: Was I the one who shot Jack?

I guess I'll never know.

Maybe it's better that way.

It's almost 11:30 a.m. Time for another drink and watching the pretty ladies walk by again.

It's all I have left now – except for the pain.

The Things We Leave Behind

As I sit here at my ancient lap top, my internet fading out, then back in again, it's still hard for me to believe that so many of us used to be so dedicated to spending almost every spare minute we had taking part in what used to be called, "social networking."

In my hey day {which seems like a millinneum ago now} the definition of social networking was a group of close knit friends getting together – in *person* – to have a good time.

Not so much now days.

By the year 2023, the only friend I had left was my cat, Toby, who I had realized much too late had been the *best* friend I'd ever had.

He has renal failure now, so now precious time with my best friend may be limited.

Now, all I see when I glance out of my front room window are scavengers {mostly at night, under the cover of darkness} who *used* to be my friends and neighbors, but now are more or less just human vultures feeding off of a derelict world.

It wasn't like this until the 5th strain of the Covid-19 hit back in the Spring of 2023.

It hadn't taken long to wipe out 68 % of the US population, and some of the smaller, third world countries were left virtual ghost towns.

It was a horrible sight to behold; in the end, folks

were dying on the street corners, their swollen lungs filled with thick, glue-like mucous and blood.

They actually died from a type of suffocation; their lungs would fill up so full of virus-induced mucous that it had nowhere to go but out through the mouth and the nasal passages – slowly but surely cutting off their air supply and choking the person to death.

It was an ugly way to go.

My quaint little home town had ended up the same, with about 70% of the population gone now, and the few of us that were left had opted to become a recluse, only venturing out when we had to, foraging for food and water.

What few of our local citizens were left behind still hadn't figured out why we hadn't contracted the virus, but we weren't about to look a gift horse in the mouth, either.

Surprisingly, I still have electricity, running water, and internet. But for how long, well...that may be up for debate. Sooner or later, more people will die, and the luxuries we all have tended to take for granted in the past will be gone, too.

My internet has begun to cut out lately. Not very often and not for long periods of time, but still cuts out nonetheless.

And I can tell that someday, maybe even sooner than later, it will fail altogether, and then...well, I don't want to think about that right now. All I can say is, when that time comes, a lot of the survivors of the Covid-5 are gonna wish they hadn't depended on the internet so much.

But for now, I am actually glad it's still up and running, because I have a story to finish, and more on line research to conduct before it's finished.

I'd like to leave one last story behind for my children and grand children. A story of how things *used* to be, and how maybe, just by luck or sheer determination, our future generations might be able to turn things around for the better.

I hope so.

I really do.

#

The things we've left behind: it's a sad state of affairs, really.

As I sit here typing away, watching my sick cat force-feeding himself a small spoonful of tuna and listening to my ancient police scanner crackling away every few minutes, with yet another report of a Covid-5 death toll or another break in or robbery or another riot breaking out down town, it's really amazing just how fast it all went to shit.

The scavengers are always out rooting around for something to steal. Some of them are infected and but harmless otherwise and just need a little help for now; others aren't apt to be so friendly.

Can't say as I can blame them, really. How would you feel if your whole world as you once knew it was falling apart before your eyes? Or your husband or wife or kids had died from the virius, and you were all alone in the mess and had nobody you were sure you could trust to turn to?

It most definitely takes it's toll on your mind, believe me.

Been there, done that.

At the height of the Covid-5 crisis, I'd lost my Mom, my brother, and some of my Facebook "friends."

There we go with that social networking again. It helped me sell books at one point but that's the one and only positive thing I can say about it.

Plus, who is going to read your books if they're dead?

Sorry to sound cruel or uncaring, that wasn't my intention. But I am a *realist*, which means, no matter how hard something may be to swallow, I just buck up and do it, face the music and try to move on best I can.

It's all I *can* do.

\#

My best buddy isn't feeling quite up to par today.

Then again, if you're a senior kitty suffering from renal failure, playing with catnip toys or chasing mice is most likely the furthest thing from your mind on any given day.

Considering his age and current physical ailments though, he does pretty well at being self sufficient. He still bathes himself and eats by himself and even gets a little feisty now and then, but otherwise, he takes a lot of naps.

He's been throwing up a lot, has lost about 50% of his body mass, and limps around on his back paws, but he's doing his best to hang in there.

Just like yours truly.

Like I said before, it's all we *can* do.

Sometimes I'll be typing away at the keyboard and he will rub his tail against my legs and purr, and give me that sad, lost look. As I gaze deep into those pretty little brown eyes, I can almost hear what he's thinking:

Hey, dad. Not feeling too good today. I sure could use some petting and sweet talk right now. Oh, and by the way, I think I heard somebody messing around in the garage last night again. Hope they didn't take any of my canned tuna!

As I pick him up to pet him, I walk over to the kitchen window and take a peek at the garage door. Sure enough, the big padlock I had replaced has been busted, the door hanging wide open, and I can see at least one box of canned goods and some bottled water is missing.

The scavengers again.

They can still go to a store and *buy* their own food, but some of them opt to *steal* it from other people instead. Several of of our home town stores are still open for business – with revised shopping hours, of course – and at times, if some of the most popular items haven't been restocked yet, like toilet paper, water, over the counter meds and canned goods, instead of just waiting in line, folks tend to steal from others.

And pretty soon, if the internet goes down, in store purchases {computerized cash registers} and electricity and heat and AC and the utility companies will *all* go down too.

That's when you will see some *real* hell break loose.

Better hoard all you can now, folks, I think, as I place Toby down on his cat bed. He is in a deep sleep almost instantly. *Because soon enough, you might end up getting a National Guard bullet up your back side for your trouble.*

I sat back down at my computer, begin typing

away again, hoping that someday my last story will be as popular as the ones before – for their own good.

I no longer worry about making any money with my writing; I just want someone to *READ* it.

I most likely won't write much more today; I have another padlock to replace and some late afternoon shopping to do.

Wish me luck.

#

Bell's Market, a local, neighborhood grocery store that used to be an enjoyable place to shop, is now nothing more than a run-down, dilapidated brick and mortar building with iron bars on the front windows. To stand back and look at it from a distance, you'd think you were looking at one of those corner market-liquor store combos you see in East Los Angeles.

Mr Bell {I never knew his first name, can't remember why now} used to be a friendly, jovial man with a three mile smile and always had something funny to say his customers, a new joke to tell.

Now, although he still does his level best to be pleasant, you can tell it's hard for him to do so. A person can get to the point where no matter how much they may actually have to be thankful for, it doesn't seem like quite enough.

The Chinese and Covid-5 took care of that.

As I walk in, Mr Bell is standing at the register, eyeballing two punkish looking kids in the back aisle, the two punks eyeballing the cooler where Mr Bell keeps the cold beer and wine selections. They see him giving them the evil eye and scoot over toward the soda pop cooler instead, and he then speaks to me.

"How's it going, Davis?" he says, with a deep rooted, chronic lung disease type tone to his voice. He normally smoked around three packs of Lucky Strikes per day, and you could hear it as he then broke out in a loud coughing fit that made me back up a few inches.

"Same old thing, different day," I reply, glancing toward the back of the store. The two punks are checking out the candy aisle now, trying to decide between Reese's Cups or Kit Kats. "And you?"

He lit up a cigarette, coughed into his hand, and said, "Same old crap, too," glancing back at the punks again. They were walking toward the register now, with their bounty in tow; two bottles of luke warm grape soda and Kit Kats. I would have preferred Reeses myself, but...the new generation, what do they know?

The taller punk has pink, spiked hair and is wearing all black, even his floppy tennis shoes. He has long pink stripes on his black jeans too. He looks like he swallowed a pink and black hand grenade.

The other kid is wearing a t-shirt emblazoned with the words COVID 5 SUCKS. I can't argue with him on that point.

They pay for their purchases with pocket change and walk out jamming to some song only they can hear, most likely death metal or punk rock, playing air guitar and bass. They look so oblivious to everything going on around them, and suddenly found myself being envious of that.

"Mr Bell," I say, shaking my head, "Got any bottled water or Dinty Moore beef stew left? I got hit again last night."

Shaking his head in disgust, he says, "Yep. In the

back room, past the bathroom. You know where it is by now. But don't use the shitter, it's stopped up again."

I nod my understanding and head toward the back room, all the while thinking about those two punk kids who seemed so oblivious to everything around them, young and rebellious and not a care in the world.

But those days, for me, are now long ago and far away.

#

On the way back home, around dusk, I catch a glimpse of a small group of scavengers in the distance.

It's almost dusk now. They always start gathering around dusk.

Gathering to make their plans for the evening. Then again, it doesn't take too much planning just to break into homes and storage sheds and steal food and water and whatever else suits them at the time.

Like my *memories*.

When I was left alone here to take over the family home, there were so many boxes of family records and heirlooms and photo albums...you name it, it was there.

That is, until some clowns broke in one night and, pissed off that they couldn't find anything of value, lit a match to some of it and set it on fire.

Inside some of those boxes were family photos, priceless to me but meant nothing to them.

All those photo memories *gone*.

As it was, I had forgotten what my family's voices sounded like, so to see their photos burned, it was almost unbearable – and infuriating.

Luckily, I had a small fire extinguisher in the

kitchen cabinet and made it out there in time to save some of my other treasures, but none of what was left could ever hold a candle to what I lost.

That thought was running through my mind now, as I watched the group of scavengers draw closer by the second.

I wanted to *hurt* them.

Or worse.

They always seemed to know just where to look for me. I'd walk into a liquor store to buy cigarettes and beer, and when I came out, there would be at least five or six of them waiting for me. Hands always outstretched, that look of hunger in their faces.

That look of *hopelessness*.

I had to admit, I'd seen that look too, before, when I looked into my own bathroom mirror.

But my empathy for them didn't make up for that fire or the break- ins or the constant harrassment.

A lot of them had just *given up*.

Torn and grimy fingers, filthy skin, tattered clothes. Their eyelids dark and greasy, the eyes dead and empty. Sometimes, I'd slide right past them, and incredibly, they wouldn't touch me. They'd slip by like oil, dark and silent. I was glad. I'd never be able to wash away the filth if they touched me.

Or worse yet, any dormant Covid-5 germs that might decide to wake up.

Today, they suddenly took a u-turn and walked toward the nearby railroad tracks. For what reason I can't figure out, unless they have decided to finally blow this pop stand and move on to greener pastures – wherever that may be.

If so, I wish them luck.

At times, I wish I could catch the last train to Clarksville, too.

But for now, I have to finish my story.

#

After putting my canned goods in the pantry this time, and replacing the padlock on the garage door { I opted for a much larger, sturdy lock this time around} I sat on thr front porch in the dark to watch the festivities.

It was the same almost every night; drinking beer and watching the bums stroll by. All up and down the street; empty driveways, a few abandoned cars on the street, their sides rusting, lights broken, windsheilds spiderwebbed with cracks. Trash and leaves littered the curbs.

They have all but given up, and it most likely won't be long before they do that too.

That's when you have to be *extra* careful with the way you conduct your own life.

Toby sits in my lap, purring and keeping one eye open, his perky little ears twitching each and every time he hears one of them coming. He's like my little security guard. His built in, acute sense of hearing and smell come in handy these days.

It seems to me like there are more and more of them each day, too.

More of them having given up – just like their own government had given up on them back in 2020.

Now homeless, forgotten, and expendable, they have no real physical address to send any relief to, and not that our current lawmakers would do so now, anyway.

Toby begins to stir now, his little claws digging ever so slightly into my right thigh. I see the faces of the bums, waving at me with their grimy fingers and smiling at me with their unshaven, greasy jowls.

The skanky women with dark eyes beckoned, the stoic men with their oily hair and heavy smell gesturing invitingly. I recognized one of them; a man who used to live only two houses down.

He used to borrow my lawn mower.

Toby hisses and growls at them, and I decide it's time to go back inside and feed him and get back to work on my story.

#

One good thing {if you can actually look at it as a "good" thing} about this situation is, if the internet does shut down soon, I will have enough first-hand research material available to me just sitting on my front porch to finish my story.

It has been said that the best way to write non fiction is to "write what you know," so I guess I have that aspect of the situation covered.

Still, I can't help but think about the way things *used* to be.

You would think by now that I would have resigned myself to the fact there is absolutely nothing I can do about my current dilemma, but it's not always that easily acceptable to me.

I sit here every day and every night, my mind filled with visions of the world before Covid 19, and Covids 2 thru 5.

As I sit here typing away again, I glance out the

living room window and watch what's left of the world *completely* fall apart around me, and, in my mind, replace those visions with happy ones.

I can close my eyes and see my family and I sitting at the kitchen table and eating good food and joking and laughing. I see Toby, plump and healthy, in the corner greedily gobbling up some tuna platter.

I can see myself on a warm sunny day, mowing the grass and watering the flowers and sitting on the front steps sipping a bottle of spring water as I watch my neighbors across the street having a block party, the smell of grilled hotdogs and burgers wafting on the warm summer breeze.

I can see myself, once healthy and happy and looking forward to writing the "next big novel," before my health began to fail me at the age of 58. High blood pressure, irregular heartbeat, back trouble, depression. You name it, I've got it.

What's *really* sad is, that's a "normal" day in my life now.

#

Toby wasn't doing well this morning.

I woke up to find him throwing up what little food he'd consumed at breakfast. He does that a lot now. He also has trouble making it to his litter box and has accidents on the carpet. He's so thin, too.

It's so hard to sit back and watch this everyday. Not knowing how much longer the only – and best – friend I have may be gone. I know it's the "natural order" of things, but it doesn't make it any easier.

I clean up the mess and place Toby in his cat bed

and get back to work on my story.

#

One good thing about my current situation. My house is paid off, and my utilities don't amount to much, considering they don't work half the time.

This last week, the local utility companies informed us by social media {Facebook, no less} that out power and water, in the near future, would be "rationed" for now. I'm already rationing my food and water {and beer} and now I have to ration the power that keeps it fresh enough to eat and drink.

I had been sober for 16 years when Covid 5 came along, but after that, if I didn't have some type of substance to help me forget how shitty my day was going, I would have lost control of my faculties.

Bad thing about it was, it was only a temporary solution to a permanent problem.

Although I've managed to cut back to three beers a day now, it's a bad habit to get into after sixteen years of sobriety, having it handy, right there in the icebox, to abuse if my days get too unbearable.

I'm hoping – and *praying*, mostly – that day never comes.

I've got a story to finish.

#

Toby passed away during the night.

I found him this morning, laying at the foot of my bed, where he'd curled up last night by my feet, wanting to be close to me.

It has been said that cats have sort of a "sixth sense" about some things, and I believe that. I think that Toby, in what he knew were the last moments of his life, wanted to be as close to me as possible, and not being to wake me up {I had guzzled a lukewarm beer and topped it off with a sleeping pill} he had snuggled up at my feet and fallen askeep for the last time.

And I wasn't even awake to say goodbye.

I wasn't even awake {sober} enough to hold him in my arms and comfort him.

Hug him and tell him how much I will always love him and miss him and never forget our times together.

But it's too late for that now, isn't it?

So goes the story of my life.

The story I must now finish, in memory of my best friend.

#

But, first things first.

I must give my best buddy a proper burial.

As I looked around the house for something to place him in – I didn't want to just toss him in a trash bag – I suddenly realized just how many items a family could store over the decades, but the item you need the most, such as an old cardboard box big enough for a kitty or a wooden box *cannot* be found.

So, as much as I hated to do it, I placed him inside of a 13 gallon trash bag, tossed in some lime powder to keep the stray animals {and the scavengers} away, tossed in one of his favorite catnip toys, and buried him about two feet down.

As I was digging his grave, I found myself cursing everyone I could blame this on; our past two Presidents, the Chinese, the money hungry power mongers, the scavengers, and anyone else I could think of from the grade school bully to the guy who borrowed my socket set and never returned it.

At the time, reeling from heartache and bawling my eyes out, it had never occurred to me that in the natural order of things, even our best kitty and canine buddies also grow old and pass away, just like we do.

At the time, I would have gladly given my own life to save his.

What did I have to live for, anyway?

Then the answer came to me like a whisper on the wind; *You have to finish your story, my best friend. Don't give up now, I'm here with you, you just can't see me.*

I'll always believe it was Toby I heard whispering to me.

You have to believe in *something*, right?

#

After the burial and a few silent prayers, I went back inside, took a *quick* shower {gotta ration the water!} and got back to work on my story.

As I sat there typing away, for some reason {I hadn't thought about this person in at least thirty years} an old girlfriend came to mind, a girl I had a massive crush on as a teenager.

I guess when a person has been locked away in their own little sad world as long as I have, your whole life slowly but surely flashes before your eyes. Today, it was in the vision of a girl named Elnora.

Her voice was music; angelic and softer than silk. Yet from that first moment I met her I sensed great sadness. She exuded an undertone of weariness and despair, as if some tragedy in her past had irreparably damaged her very soul. Her eyes seemed to bear the weight of a millennium's tears.

They were as green as the rich green grass beneath her feet and sparkled like emeralds, but when she felt threatened, they darkened to dull obsidian like the sad vision of a broken china doll. It was in those eyes I first glimpsed the vastness of her pain; it was in those eyes I saw my destiny.

She was bright and hopeful and dark and endlessly deep. She was fire and ice and everything in between, and I held her gaze, felt the coldness of her touch, and listened to her sadness.

I loved her from the moment I saw her.

Then she vanished like a ghost.

It happened a lot in one's youth, friends and girlfriends both coming and going as routinely as one would brush their teeth or drink their morning coffee.

Young love – or infatuation, as my mother would have called it – was just part of growing up back in those days and done so much more innocently than the generations that followed my own. It was like magic between two teenagers who thought they were in love; like a romance novel come to life, a romantic movie with a happy ending.

But the hurt, the genuine heartache was still there

just the same, and especially when the object of your affections had seemed to have vanished without a trace. *Did she and her family just move away? If so, why wouldn't she say goodbye to me?*

At that moment, all thoughts of considering myself the ladies' man of our motley crew had vanished as well, and I was left with a mystery, one I intended to solve regardless of the risk to life and limb, or to my curfew. To me, this was so much more than a simple case of infatuation or puppy love, it was a mission, one to find a ghost, a supernaturally beautiful ghost that would come back to haunt me in my dreams for many years to come.

Thirty years, to be exact; I never saw her again – unless it was in my dreams.

Or in my last story.

#

My last story.

That sounds more than a little depressing to me right now. It's hard – almost impossible, really – to believe that this might be my last story.

But it's quite obvious that it will be. With the current rationing of power, and the internet fading in and out {mostly out now} it may not be much longer until I can't finish it, so I better make the best of the time I have left.

As I sit here today, glancing out the window at Toby's grave, so many people and memories come flooding back in now.

I can close my eyes and I can see Elnora and I, the two of us holding hands and walking through the city park, laughing and giggling and being so madly in love we just knew it would never end.

I guess for me, it never did, and I didn't realize it until now.

I see myself as a child and my Mom at the city beach, playing in the water and building sand castles and blushing as pretty little girls walked by.

I can see my old friends and I at the park in the summer, soaking up the sun and washing and waxing their cars. In the distance, I can hear the old Blue Oyster Cult song, "Don't Fear the Reaper," playing on someone's 8-track player, and I can't help but realize how befitting that song is now, almost 46 years later, the reaper having come in the form of Covid 5.

I can see so many wonderful things with my eyes closed, but when I open them, all that's left is ugliness and hatred and dark days and death.

And my best friend's grave.

I think I need to take a break for now.

#

I went outside to toss something in the trash {the city trash collectors are on strike now, so I don't know why I even bother to place it in a trash can} and upon coming back inside, I suddenly felt very weak, almost fatigued, so I went to the bathroom to take a look at myself in the mirror.

The pallor of my skin is terrible, almost ghost like, and I have dark circles under my eyes.

Then *it* happened.

I went into a coughing *fit*, that kind of painful, deep rooted cough, that almost doubles you over from the force of it all.

I kept coughing and coughing until I thought I was literally going to cough up something I needed, and when I finally stopped, my breathing was so labored I was scared shitless.

But *it* wasn't done with me yet.

I suddenly began choking, and I could feel something coming up in my throat, like that feeling you get when you're about to be sick, but it wasn't bile that came up.

It was *blood*.

That's when I knew my time was most definitely limited as far as finishing my story.

#

It's really funny how our brains work, you know?

We all have that so called "memory palace," where we store all of our happy memories; then we have that dark spot where we keep our unhappy ones; then we have that little voice in our head that tells us to do things that aren't good for us, or vice-versa.

I'm sure you know what I'm talking about.

But as human beings so often do, we seem to take these things for granted, yet, when you've just coughed up bloody mucous in the bathroom sink, the only thing you can think of is sitting at your computer, to work on a story that people might never read.

But, you hang in there, don't you?

Because you know, deep inside your own memory palace, this is the *only* thing you have left to live for.

#

After cleaning myself up a bit and brushing my teeth, I went outside to sit on the back porch and have a cup of coffee {the alcohol I have in the house doesn't seem too appealing right now} and rest a bit before getting back to work on my "magnum opus."

At least I *hope* it ends up being an important piece of literature. I'd hate to think I sat here all this time, spending my last days on a story that nobody takes the time to read.

I was going to use social media to get it out the masses quicker, but as of six months ago, Twitter, Parler, My Space are all down, Facebook being the only one left, and fades in and out quite a bit, too. I bet that pisses off a lot of the hard core "Face-boogies."

How am I going to accomplish this seemingly impossible task?

So many questions, so few real answers, and so little time left now.

I think I need another break for now, and take a walk to clear my head.

#

I decided to take a walk down to Lester Talbot's place.

Lester is an older fella {as he says, "older than dirt"} that lives down the road, close to the Wabash River, who used to be a local farmer – and moonshiner.

He's a real character, old Lester. Always has a new {and corny} joke to tell, always seems like he's in a good mood, and always flashing thast big gap-toothed grin of his to add to the comedic aspect of the conversation.

I *needed* a good laugh, so I took a walk down to see him.

When I rounded the corner of Sixth Street Road, I could see him already, sitting on the front porch, as usual, in his ancient rocking chair, rocking back and forth and puffing on his corn cob pipe.

He told me once that his late wife, Erma, had talked him out of smoking cigarettes for his health's sake. He'd taken up chewing after he'd quit smoking, just like he'd taken up smoking after he'd quit drinking his homemade shine at Erma's request, who'd told him the shine had made him 'ornery.' In hindsight – now that he'd sobered up – he'd tend to agree with her.

As I walked up to the porch, he flashed that big, gap toothed grin of his, and before he could even say hi, I could see that he was now missing even more teeth, and the ones he had left were caked with dried blood.

Folded up neatly in his breast pocket was a blood stained napkin, too, so it was now official: the only real buddy I had left in the neighborhood had the Covid 5, too.

Like two peas in a pod.

Or, like two dead men walking, depending on how you wanted to look at it.

Either way, our mutual prognosis was very grim at best.

"Howdy there, good buddy," he said as I reached the bottom of the porch steps. "Long time, no see."

I sat down on the next to the bottem step and lit a cigarette – as if I really needed one. "Hey, Lester, you old fart. How ya been?"

He stopped rocking and leaned out to take a better look at me. "Damn, son," he said, shaking his head. "You've definitely looked better."

"I've felt a lot better, too," I said, glancing out at his small vegetable garden. It was old and shriveled up an dead. Just like I'd be feeling soon enough. "You don't look so good yourself."

He leaned back again. Took a deep breath, and coughed a couple of times. He said, "Yep. That damn Covid 5 finally got me. I knew it was only a matter of time. That Covid 5, it likes us older folks. We're a lot easier to kill."

"It likes us younger folks too," I said, crushing out my cigarette with my boot. "Covid 5 is definitely not a racist virus, we are all equally worthless."

He sat up again. "Oh no, not *you* too. I'm so sorry buddy, I really am."

I forced a smile. "Me too, old buddy, me too."

Lester forced a smile too, and said, "Well, good buddy, I guess we're like two peas in a pod now, huh?"

Or like two dead men walking, I thought, but didn't say so. Instead, I changed the subject. "Lester, do you still have any of that famous apple pie moonshine you used to make? I could use a drink right now."

He smiled and whispered , "Just between you and me? I have *one* quart jar left. Erma never knew anything about it, though. It made me feel sorta guilty after she'd passed, ya know?"

I nodded in understanding, but said, "Well, Lester, I have the feeling that, under our present circumstances, she wouldn't mind at all."

#

After a few sips of Lester's famous shine and some friendly banter, Lester had suddenly grown very tired, well, fatigued, actually, and had gone back inside to take a nap.

Hopefully not a dirt nap, but at his age, you never know. Then again, I'm only 60 years old, and by the time I get back home, I might take a peek in the mirror and look just like him.

Covid 5 worked *fast*.

I hated to leave Lester in the shape he was in, but what could I possibly do for him? The hardest part was saying goodbye. I knew deep down I'd never see him again – at least alive, anyway.

But I had to get back to *finish the story*.

That may sound terribly selfish so my readers, but I'm trying to finish something that could be very, very important to future generations.

Whether it will be or not may remain to be seen, but I'm not giving up now.

This damned Covid 5 isn't going to defeat me now. No way.

#

On the way home, I see a large group of scavengers on both sides of the street.

I stop walking, duck behind a large oak tree, and check them out. The large groups are always good for a laugh, too.

I see one of them, a tall guy with a scraggly, flea

infested beard and thick, coke bottle glasses, staggering down the street like a drunk. He's wearing a Western style hat and an old, stained Covid 4 mask around his neck like a bandana. *The cowboy from hell.*

Idiot.

Too many people not obeying the mask mandate is what helped the virus to spread.

One group across the street from my house stops, huddles like a football team, no doubt planning on what to do next – or who to prey on next. They briefly glance toward my house, and then walk away. Maybe word has gotten around that the guy who lives there is crazy, talks to himself and drinks too much and whose best friend is a dead cat.

Fine with me.

I wait a few seconds, until that group passes by, then I begin walking at a snail's pace, as not to let anyone on the street know I'm not quite as desperate as the rest of them just yet.

Or am I?

#

About a block from the house, a huge group of them comes around the opposite corner, about fifty of them at least.

I freeze, not moving a muscle. But not because I'm necessarily frightened by them, but by what – or whom - I see right in the middle of the crowd.

It's my parents, and my brother. All three long since dead, skeletal and ghastly.

All three holding out their arms to me, beckoning to me, like they're telling me it's alright now. *It's okay,*

Davis.

You did your best and now it's time to come home. God knows you tried, too.

Then they were gone.

It was all in my mind.

What's left of it.

Then I remembered something my mom told me as a child; *if you're ever scared by something you see, if it's really scary and you just know it's not real, close your eyes, count to five and open them.*

So I did.

They were gone.

Goodbye, and I love you. I thought. *But don't worry, you'll see me soon enough.*

#

As I neared my house, keeping within the tree line to stay at least partially hidden, it happened.

The street lights in my neighborhood suddenly went out, with a big POP! sound, and I was left in total darkness. I glanced at my wristwatch to see it was already past dusk.

The power! I thought, my heart and mind both racing.

My *INTERNET!*

I ran toward my house as fast as I could, pushing scavengers out of the way and jumping a fence and bursting through my back door, tripping over my own feet and landing face first on the hard wood floor.

The last thing I remember before I blacked out was hearing a loud, bone-crunching sound...and then, total darkness again.

#

The loud, bone crunching sound had been my nose breaking.

I woke up in a pool of blood and my nose cockeyed at an almost impossible angle, but I was still alive.

And unfortunately, still in total darkness.

I managed to stand up, weaving a little bit, wrapped a small wash rag around my face to soak up blood, then went down into the basement to fuel up the gas powered generator.

A few minutes later, drinking a beer and popping some extra strength Tylenol, I was at my computer working on my story.

#

The pain in my nose was so severe, I felt I had to do something a tad bit more extreme than popping Tylenol.

I walked into the pantry, retrieved the bottle of single malt scotch I'd had for so many years {I had kept it around to prove to myself I wouldn't open it, fat lot of good that did} and walked into the bathroom, took several big sips from the bottle, took a deep breath before placing my hands on both sides of my nose, with my fingers pressed against the fractured area, and pressed down on both sides at the same time.

The pain was so excruciating, I almost passed out again, and leaned against the sink, looking at my reflection in the mirror.

It looked better, and hurt somewhat less, but it

was still swollen and bruised. *Good enough*, I thought, taking another sip of scotch. *Back to work I go.*

I hadn't been sitting at my computer for long before the internet began fading in and out again, and I began to panic, the sweat pouring off my forehead and my stomach tied up in knots.

It faded back in.

And out.

And back in again.

I began typing away again, making so many typos and grammical errors it was pathetic.

I finally managed to calm down, the scotch kicking in now, I slowed down, taking my time.

Then it happened.

My PC screen lit up real bright, made a loud popping sound, and the internet was *gone*.

A pop up box in the corner of the screen confirmed my worst fears for me: **INTERNET DISCONNECTED.**

I glanced around the room just to be sure; the icebox was still humming and the lights were on, so I knew it was gone for sure.

So close, but yet so far.

I took another drink of scotch.

#

It was like I'd slipped into a drunken blackout.

One minute, I was sitting at my computer with tears streaming down my face, and the next minute I found myself lying on the kitchen floor.

I struggled to my feet and glanced around the room again through bleary eyes; the PRINTER.

I could print it out, and leave one copy here, and other copies around town. At least the story would be seen that way.

I hope.

#

The next morning, after gulping down black coffee instead of booze, I'd finally sobered up enough to take a long, lukewarm shower and change my clothes.

After force feeding myself some very bland oatmeal {ran out of sugar or syrup} I sat down at my computer, turned on the power to my printer, and opened up the story file.

It was hard to believe that I'd come this far with my story, under seemingly impossible odds and delays.

A 28 page, magnum opus of heartache, memories, and I am hoping good advice for future generations.

My very *heart and soul* went into this story, and if it benefits just *one* person {the *right* person, that is} it would have been worth it.

But I'm hoping I reach as many people as possible.

Time to start printing.

#

I covered most of my neighbrohood today; utility poles, store fronts, and even placing them on parked cars. Any place I could think of that someone *coherent*, someone the Covid 5 virus hasn't damaged yet, might find them. I know there are still folks out there are...well, half way *normal*, so surely someone will find them, take the time to read them, if not only for something to do when they get bored.

I am hoping my story won't be boring; the journey here was anything *but* boring.

I'm *so* tired now.

My face hurts, ny chest hurts, and I've been coughing up blood again.

I think I will retire early tonight, get some much needed rest, and hope I wake up in the morning.

Just one more day, God, okay?

Just one more sunny day, to hear the birds singing and the crickets chirping and maybe, just maybe, see my kids again.

Just one more day, Lord.

Amen.

#

In the middle of the night, my old radio began crackling away, and I heard bits and pieces of the lastest news:

The border wall finally came down. Since then, even *more* illegal aliens have invaded the US, and the crime rate has gone up 43% already.

The current value of the US dollar – if it even matters now – is down to 35 cents.

The current President has gone into hiding – along with his other corrupt co-conspirators.

The Chinese have cut off *all* trade with the US, and are talking WAR – as if the Covid wasn't enough.

The National Guard is out in full force – but are still getting pushed back beyond their barriers, by Antifa, BLM, and, of course, the ever present scavengers.

I can't take any more, and reach down and yanked

the radio cord out of the wall, and throw it across the room.

Back to sleep I go.

#

I woke up to a cloudy day.

No birds singing, crickets chirping, or knocks at my door.

Maybe the scavengers ate them.

The birds I mean.

Yes...*the things we leave behind.*

You should never mess with mother nature, fate, or destiny.

Or God's own master plan.

It's too bad that our own government didn't think about that until it was too late.

I rise from bed late today, and start out with a bottle of heavy red wine but move on to a burning whiskey that seems to set my eyes and brain on fire.

One thing left to do now.

After coughing up some more blood.

I print the story out one last time, staple it together, and leave it on my desk, right in front of my computer, so if someone does happen to find it, at least ONE person will see it, and maybe, just maybe, will pass it on to someone else.

And so on.

I was hoping my kids would find it, but I haven't heard from them in weeks. Or is it months? I'm not really sure anymore; I think the Covid 5 has begun robbing me of my memory altogether.

Except for the times, of course, I have another

nightmare. I guess Covid 5 doesn't rob you of those, huh?

I'm not worried too much; if all else fails, I still have some single malt scotch and my .22 caliber pistol to take care of that.

But for now, I climb back into bed and take another sleeping pill so that I won't have to remember my dreams.

David Boyer is a Christian, a multi-genre writer, a true crime buff, and the author of several coming of age novellas, numerous horror and scifi stories, as well as the author of numerous essays including the subjects of government corruption, Christianity, bullying, and cyber-stalking.

He lives in Vincennes, Indiana, with his cat, Holly Jean, who now serves as his copy editor by jumping on the computer keyboard when he's not looking.

Books: {Non-fiction}
True crime:
Small Town Murder: True Crime Stories From Knox County, Indiana
Murder In the Hoosier Heartland: Infamous Indiana Murderers & Fledgling Serial Killers
Murder & Mayhem In the Hoosier Heartland: Mysterious Disappearances & Bizarre Murders In Indiana
The Blitz: A Rape Victim's Story
Vanished In Vincennes: the Mysterious Disappearance and Death Of Dolores Oliver
47 Years of Hell: The Dolores Oliver Murder: Still Unsolved
Small Town Murder In Knox County, Indiana: Hate Crimes, Witch Hunts, and A Definitive List of Indiana Serial Killers
The Guy In The Blue Shirt

Non-fiction: {paranormal, bio & memoir}
Haunted Heartland: Haunted Hoosiers Tell Their Ghost Stories
Strange Happenings In the Hoosier Heartland
I Remember When, In Vincennes…Volume 1
Growing Up In Vincennes – Volumes 2 – 5
The Time of Our Lives: Growing Up Cool In Vincennes, Indiana

Essays:
Bullying: the Road to Recovery and Forgiveness
Privacy In the Age of the Internet: How Sexting and Sharing Private Photos Can lead To Cyber-Stalking
Once An Alcoholic, Always An Alcoholic? The Cold Hard Truth About Our Addictions
Travesties of Jutice: Flaws In Our Legal System That Imprison the Innocent
Will the REAL Christian Please Stand Up?
Racism in the 21st Century: ALL Lives Matter
Conflicted Souls: How the Man In Black Saved My Life
Crossing the Rainbow Bridge: Saying Goodbye To Our Beloved Pets

Books: {Fiction}
Mystery, Indiana
Human Sawdust
Mutant Moon and Other Stories
Lucid Nightmares – A Collection of Short Fiction

Stories: {Long fiction, novellas}
Mystery, Indiana
The Mind of Luther Biggs
LUTHER

Jenny
Lester Talbot and His Magic Eye
Beautiful Ghosts
Pretty Flamingo
Jack and Norma Jean
The Things We Leave Behind – Volumes 1 – 3
Ghosts of Summer
Gardens
Claustrophobia
The Cemetery Artist
Brain Pie
Beast
The Jailhouse Movie Star
Easy Pickings
The Dominant Thumb
Joyride
The Maverick
Freak
Grandma's Gooseberry Pie
Dancing With the King
Always In My Heart
Hillbilly Moonshine Zombies
Home
Sheva
A Debt Repaid In Full
The Enlightening Darkness
The Good Neighbor
Wander
The Hungry Ones
A Gunfighter's Legacy
Dead Man's Hand
Inhuman Experiments – Part 1, 2, and 3
Jennifer

Spider Bait
Poor Larry
Creepy Crawl
They Call Me The Wolf
Welcome To Deadman's Gulch
Uncle Marty
The Guy In The Blue Shirt
Mutant Moon
Elnora's Eyes
Goodnight, My Love
Wildflowers
Blue Moonlight
Black Midnight
Two Men, Sitting On The Front Porch, Talking About The End Of the World
True Love Never Dies: An Apocalyptic Love Story
Save Me
Shadow Dolls
The Ghosts Of Halloween
Restless Hearts

Other books by David Boyer
Now available on Lulu.com

There are certain places, certain *societies*, that are hidden away from the rest of the world – and with good reason. A small, nameless town deep in the back woods of West Virginia is one such place; long hidden away from the rest of the world in order to keep it's dark secrets in tow.

Little do the local residents know, they are about to be invaded by two men who will threaten the very existence of the small town, and possibly expose their dark secrets to the rest of the outside world, and, in the process, expose dark, unholy horrors that the outside world couldn't even imagine in their worst nightmares.

Even small towns can harbor big secrets.

Jake Collins, the former Deputy Sheriff in Deadman's Gulch, Texas, knows this all too well.

Since his wife was killed in a hit and run "accident" years ago, and the case covered up to hide the identity of the real culprit, Jake has found out the hard way that some of the secrets in that town – including the mystery behind his wife's death – are sometimes better off left dead and buried.

But none of that mattered to Jake now.

He was back here for one purpose and one

purpose only; to kill the culprit in cold blood – and God help anyone who got in his way.

An eye for an eye.

A tooth for a tooth.

And plenty of bloody mayhem to go around.

9 798224 653669